Darkness *falls upon* Pemberley

SUSAN ADRIANI

WHITE
SOUP
PRESS

Darkness Falls Upon Pemberley

Copyright © 2013, 2012 by Susan Adriani
Cover and interior design by CloudCat Design
Cover image: *A Young Lady* by Mary Green, née Byrne, ca 1845

First paperback edition 2013

ISBN-13: 978-0615806747
ISBN-10: 0615806740

Published by White Soup Press

Visit us at www.whitesouppress.com
Meet your favorite Austenesque authors at www.austenauthors.net
Susan Adriani's website: www.thetruthaboutmrdarcy.weebly.com

10   9   8   7   6   5   4   3   2   1

For Rebecca H. & Rebecca Z.,
two constant beacons of inspiration,
whether they realize it or not.

*P*rologue

Many things are rarely as they seem. That much he knew. It had taken but one evening spent in her company to understand she was like no woman he'd ever encountered. There was something in her air, in her manner of speaking, in the way she moved and laughed that prevented him from dismissing her as commonplace. Miss Morton, Miss Redgrave, Miss Bingley—and dozens upon dozens of other ladies of the London *ton*, with their simpering attention, banal conversation, and exhausting single-mindedness— were commonplace; not Miss Elizabeth Bennet.

Though they'd been acquainted less than a fortnight, Darcy had become thoroughly enamoured with her. For a man used to being his own lord and master, the development of such a strong attachment was unsettling, especially when nothing—not even the inferiority of her situation and connexions—had proven a powerful enough deterrent against the spell she'd woven.

Her intelligence was formidable and had fanned the flames of his admiration with as much ease as the teasing curve of her lips had coaxed his smile. Her wit and vivacity garnered equal veneration, as did the subtle sway of her hips whenever she entered a room, or danced a reel, or strode confidently through the countryside as though she hadn't a care in the world.

Her complexion was flawless; her skin pale and pure, and her dark, glossy locks—whether perceived by the glow of a wax taper or the natural light of day—appeared, in Darcy's opinion, more lustrous than the finest bolts of silk.

His fingers itched to caress her cheek, her bare shoulder, the supple swell of her breast. The hours he'd spent thinking of her, fantasizing about her, wondering whether her body might be as responsive to his touch as he'd imagined had become too numerous to count. Darcy wanted to lose himself in her eyes and become immersed in her scent. He wanted to brush his lips against the shell of her ear and whisper his deepest desires.

He longed to make her breath quicken.

He longed to make her blush.

The thought of her blush alone was enough to make his pulse race. The idea of seeing Elizabeth with a flushed countenance; of feeling the quickening of her heartbeat, and knowing it was by his hands, did sinful things to him—dangerous things; things that, as a gentleman, he could ill-afford to act upon with any lady, never mind one so utterly lovely, innocent, and trusting as Miss Elizabeth Bennet of Hertfordshire.

With an exhalation, he closed his eyes and attempted to put a rein on his heightened emotions. The last thing in the world that ought to be on Darcy's mind was engaging in a flirtation, however deeply felt on his part; especially when his beloved younger sister was almost completely alone in the world, in isolation at his ancestral estate in Derbyshire: Pemberley.

He scowled, frustrated and bitter about the cruel situation in which they now found themselves. A few months ago Georgiana was innocent and whole, completely unspoilt by the world and any evil that dwelled in its shadows; and Darcy, though he wouldn't go so far as to say he was happy, neither had he been miserable.

But at Ramsgate everything had changed.

Yes, he had arrived in time to save Georgiana, but not soon enough to prevent her current state, or eliminate her suffering. And though he and his cousin Colonel Fitzwilliam had acted swiftly to conceal her and exact retribution on the one responsible, in the end their actions were too little, too late. Georgiana was ever altered. Never again would she be the same gentle girl they'd known and loved, and yet, neither would she ever be anything else.

Darcy doubted that any man—even his good-natured friend Charles Bingley—was capable of enough selflessness and compassion to marry her. The fact that she could claim a dowry of £30,000 and ties to an ancient, though untitled family would carry no weight should Georgiana foolishly choose to confide her story to an unsuspecting suitor. In fact, the repercussions would be nothing short of catastrophic.

Should Darcy decide to take a wife the outcome would most likely be equally disastrous. Deception of any sort had always been abhorrent to him; therefore, he knew he could never in good conscience enter into an engagement without absolute honesty and full disclosure. But what if, after revealing all, his intended refused to accept or even tolerate his beloved sister? Darcy could never, *would* never disown Georgiana, but what if the woman he chose to spend his life with demanded it of him? What if, in a fit of anger and disgust, she told the world his sister's darkest secret?

Perhaps he would do better to remain a bachelor than take such a risk.

His conscience, however, whispered that Elizabeth Bennet would never make such a demand of him; that her heart was too kind and her spirit too generous to behave so cruelly, either toward Georgiana or himself.

For half an hour his mind entertained impossible scenarios. Should Elizabeth ever consent to visit Pemberley Darcy could carefully introduce them. Georgiana, he knew, would take one look at Elizabeth and adore her. He was equally certain that Elizabeth, after seeing the sweetness in his sister, would undoubtedly feel the same.

But would such fledgling sentiments, however tender, survive once Elizabeth understood what his sister had so recently become? What Georgiana would always remain in the eyes of Society—nay, in the eyes of the entire world?

Darcy swallowed thickly. Would Elizabeth shun them? Or would her inherent compassion prevail, even in so hopeless a case as theirs? His practical side knew no connexion between them—either with his sister or himself—should even be considered, never mind attempted. But there was a part of him that had grown undeniably selfish, especially given the sacrifices he'd made for his sister's sake. Was it so awful of him to wish to know such happiness as Elizabeth could bring? Would it be so terrible of him to attempt it?

He exhaled roughly and ran slightly shaking hands through his hair. It was October, he was settled comfortably at Netherfield, and, by Georgiana's insistence, at leisure until Christmas. *There is no need for rashness,* he told himself, *in any quarter. At least not at present…*

His late father had been a firm believer that impetuosity was a mark of weakness in a man; weakness of mind and weakness of character. Until a few months ago Darcy had staunchly believed it, too, but no more. It was his impatience to see her that had ultimately enabled him to rescue Georgiana from the arms of evil. Perhaps a bit of impetuosity could now rescue Darcy as well.

One

The autumn wind blew in fitful gusts, rattling branches and sweeping fallen leaves into chaotic frenzy as nighttime settled over Hertfordshire. Inside Lucas Lodge several roaring fires blazed brightly in the drawing room hearths, welcome beacons for those who'd braved the sharp chill of evening in order to make merry with their neighbours.

"I trust you are enjoying your stay in Hertfordshire, Mr. Darcy."

Though many of Sir William's guests had been vying for her attention, she was speaking to him, and Darcy was beyond delighted. "I thank you, yes. Though I've been here but a few weeks, Miss Bennet, I've found much to admire in Hertfordshire."

"I'm gratified to hear it, sir, for I've often observed that those used to the bustling excitement and endless attractions of Town have a tendency to declare our humble society confined and unvarying. Your lack of expeditiousness is refreshing."

Elizabeth's impertinence was far more welcome to Darcy than the insipid words regularly uttered by the women of the *bon ton*. As always, she looked completely and unwittingly lovely. The rich, chocolate colour of her gown, but a few shades lighter than her hair, presented a stunning contrast to her snow-white skin. Darcy's eyes lingered appreciatively on each exquisite inch exposed to him. The elegant column of her neck, unadorned except for a delicate garnet cross, he found especially enticing. It would have pleased him infinitely more, however, to see her without any decoration. Her natural beauty was enough. She needed no further embellishment.

A mournful air, coerced by awkward fingers on Lady Lucas' pianoforte jolted Darcy from his admiration. Chagrinned, he forced his eyes upward until they met Elizabeth's and cleared his throat.

"While that is undoubtedly the case with some," he replied, "you seem to have forgotten, madam, my estate is settled far to the north, and thereby surrounded by a similar ease and solitude. Though I confess to missing the theatre and museums to some degree whenever I'm absent from Town, I'm afraid I cannot repine much beyond that. In fact, it has long been my observation that variety and freshness are as abundant in rural, country neighbourhoods as they are in London, if one takes the trouble to notice."

She appeared amused by his response, and arched her brow in challenge. "Shall I take that to mean you are not eager to be gone, then, Mr. Darcy? Our humble shire and its sometimes eccentric residents have yet to frighten you off? I find that interesting, indeed," she said, raising her wine glass to her lips and taking a slow sip.

"I daresay we are all of us eccentric in our own way, Miss Bennet. I am, however, exceedingly flattered to hear that you find me interesting."

"Oh," she replied, "but I have not declared *you* interesting, sir, only your stubbornness."

"You believe I am stubborn?" he cried, though his grin belied his affronted tone. "I suppose on certain subjects I am, but that I ought to be scared away by your neighbours, you must own, is a ridiculous notion. I've rarely met with pleasanter people."

"Perhaps, I've misspoken," she said archly. "Perhaps it is not the neighbours of whom you ought to be wary."

Darcy's smile slipped as he realised the irony of her implication, and felt a pang of guilt. Though this woman had most definitely taken him by surprise, and his instant, powerful attraction to her had caused him some degree of alarm initially, he'd never felt afraid of her. Discomposed by her, entranced by her, enamoured and aroused by her, yes; but certainly never afraid.

If Darcy feared anything it was losing Elizabeth's friendship because of Georgiana's unfathomable situation, but he told himself that was presently neither here nor there. For Elizabeth to learn of their troubles Darcy would have to inform her himself and, though he knew enough of her character to feel confident he could rely on Elizabeth's discretion on many matters, he had no desire to speak so openly of something so personal and painful to him; at least not when their acquaintance was still relatively new.

He could, however, speak honestly of other things, and said sincerely, "Miss Bennet, I have found your society, by far, the most satisfying of all your Hertfordshire neighbours and I'm extraordinarily grateful for your kindness in bestowing it. Surely, you cannot mean to imply that I ought to be fearful of you?"

Elizabeth's eyes sparkled with mischief and, perhaps, Darcy thought, a hint of something more. "You do not find me fearsome, sir?"

A small smile lifted the corners of Darcy's mouth as he shook his head. "I would not call you particularly fearsome, no."

"Frightening, then?" she hedged.

Darcy laughed.

Elizabeth pursed her lips in mock indignation, but her eyes, dancing with mirth, belied her pleasure.

"Tell me. Is there nothing you find even remotely intimidating about me, Mr. Darcy; nothing at all?"

He dipped his chin and shook his head with a chuckle, slowly swirling the contents of his wine glass. *Intimidating, indeed,* he thought as he brought the glass to his lips.

As satisfying as he found her playful banter, in his heart Darcy longed to have a more serious conversation with Elizabeth; an infinitely more private exchange where he'd look deeply into her eyes and confess his ever-increasing attachment to her, and perhaps—if he felt particularly bold—the ardent nature of his admiration. Now *that,* he owned, was a terrifying prospect!

While Elizabeth's eagerness to seek him out and tease him on multiple occasions had managed to convince him his suit would likely be welcome, he reminded himself this was Elizabeth Bennet before him and not some calculable lady of the *ton.* She was nothing if not unpredictable.

He'd learned very early on in their acquaintance that neither his reputed fortune, his house in Town, nor Caroline Bingley's exultant praise of Pemberley had managed to impress her, which left Darcy in unfamiliar territory. The realization that he had nothing more to recommend him but his charm was hardly a welcome one. Not only had the reticent master of Pemberley felt uncomfortable exerting himself in order to attract the interest of the opposite sex, but his reputation had never required it of him. That is, not until he'd met a certain persuasive Hertfordshire beauty.

Drawing a fortifying breath, Darcy cleared his throat and, with what he hoped was an engaging smile, gestured toward a cushioned window seat in the far corner of the room that was, for the moment, blessedly unoccupied. There, they would have more privacy from prying eyes and lose tongues. "Would you do me the honour of indulging me for a moment, Miss Bennet? I should very much like to speak with you."

"I was under the impression we were speaking," she replied as she took another sip of wine.

Darcy stared at her, momentarily caught as he awkwardly shifted his weight from one foot to the other; but when she lowered her glass he saw a familiar, teasing smile playing upon her pretty mouth and managed to relax his stance, if only a little.

"Yes," he replied sheepishly. "I suppose we are. Pray forgive my forwardness. I'm afraid I don't usually perform well to strangers and, apparently, tonight is no exception." He gestured to the room in general, overflowing with Sir William's guests. To his immense relief, every last one of them appeared to be engaged at present, and so paid them no particular attention he could discern.

In silence Elizabeth regarded him. Her teasing countenance had turned serious, the lightness between them shifting to something infinitely darker and heavier, larger than the both of them combined. He hadn't even realized he'd drawn closer to her until he felt her gloved hand upon his chest, gently stopping his advance. It was nothing more than a brief touch, but it was enough to sear his skin, even through the heavy fabric of his dress coat, waistcoat, and the fine lawn of his shirt. Darcy drew a shuddering breath and took a step backward, inwardly chastising himself for his momentary lack of decorum. He was about to stutter an apology when she spoke.

"I've noticed nothing amiss with your performance. In fact, no one admitted to the privilege of knowing you could think anything wanting."

Much like her touch, her quiet words flooded Darcy's breast with unparalleled warmth, overwhelming him, but at the same time also robbing him of what little of his reticence remained. "You, madam," he said roughly, "are no stranger. How is it that I've come to feel as though I've known you for years rather than mere weeks?"

"Perhaps you have," she replied after a moment, turning her head aside as the hint of a smile blossomed on her lips. "Perhaps we were once friends in a former lifetime, such as the Hindus believe." She glanced at him from the corner of her eye, almost nervously then, and Darcy found it impossible not to smile himself.

"Perhaps," he muttered, surprised, yet infinitely pleased by such evidence of her knowledge of the world. Elizabeth was obviously no stranger to her father's library, and in that moment Darcy couldn't help but picture her in Pemberley's library, settled comfortably before the fire as they discussed countless subjects, many of which very few ladies of his acquaintance were prepared to discuss with any level of intelligence, never mind interest.

Though Elizabeth's wine glass was nearly full he reached for it, gratified when she surrendered it willingly. Darcy set it down upon a nearby table beside his own, far emptier glass. He was about to offer her his arm and escort her to the window seat, where he had every intention of boldly confessing his ever-increasing admiration of her, when they were suddenly joined by her father. The grim, almost hostile expression on Mr. Bennet's face wiped the complacent smile from Darcy's with the efficiency of a bucket of ice cold water.

The master of Pemberley recovered quickly, however, and offered the elder gentleman a cordial inclination of his head. "Good evening to you, Mr. Bennet. How do you do?" Despite his disappointment and irritation at being thus interrupted, Darcy's tone was civil. Whether

Elizabeth's father's address would be equally so, remained to be seen.

Two

Mr. Bennet observed no pleasantries beyond a curt nod in Darcy's general direction before addressing his daughter. "I daresay you've entertained Mr. Darcy long enough, my dear. It's time to let Sir William's other guests have an opportunity to enjoy his company."

Though Mr. Bennet's volume was discreet enough that his neighbours were unlikely to overhear him, Darcy had no such difficulty, and couldn't decide whether he was more appalled by Elizabeth's father's assumption that he'd desire a reprieve from her society, or by the man's complete disregard for her sensibilities by actually giving voice to such an insinuation.

Darcy assured Mr. Bennet that nothing could be further from the truth. "As a matter of fact," he added, directing his attention to Elizabeth, "I'm unable to recall ever passing an evening so agreeably. Will you not take mercy upon me, Miss Bennet, and indulge me a while longer? I find I am loath to part ways so soon."

"You see, Papa," she said, placing her hand upon her father's arm, "all is well. There is nothing to fear."

But neither his daughter's words nor Darcy's assuaged Longbourn's master, whose disinclination to indulge the couple was evident by his rigid stance and disapproving glare. "Be that as it may," he said tightly, giving Elizabeth a pointed look, "I believe it is in everyone's best interest that Mr. Darcy rejoins his friends now. He has neglected them this evening, and I have little doubt they're regretting the loss of his society acutely. I have it on good authority that Miss Bingley, in particular, desires to see him safely returned to his party. According to Jane, she is an intimate friend of Mr. Darcy's sister, who I understand is but fifteen years old."

Abruptly Elizabeth withdrew her hand from her father's arm and turned aside her head. Darcy's keen eyes did not miss the heavy rise and fall of her breast, the hard set of her jaw, or the way her fingers curled into fists as she perceived the rest of her family on the opposite side of the drawing room, seemingly oblivious to the exchange taking place between father and daughter.

Mary, Elizabeth's middle sister, was seated primly at the pianoforte, fumbling her way through a doleful dirge while the two youngest conversed energetically with several red-coated officers. Their mother, who forever encouraged their forwardness, attended them with an indulgent smile. Bingley was with them and Elizabeth's eldest sister Jane, predictably, stood at his side. To Darcy's surprise, however, Jane's eyes were not demurely downcast as Bingley prattled on about whatever topic struck his calf-eyed fancy at the moment, but fixed intently upon Elizabeth with an expression of utmost distress.

Elizabeth raised one hand to her neck, where her trembling fingertips sought the garnet cross nestled at the hollow of her throat. She swallowed thickly, caressing the pendant in an almost methodical fashion before grasping it tightly in her fist. The expression she wore as she turned and addressed her father simmered with defiance.

"While I will always understand your concern and Jane's, and can even appreciate your interference on occasion, I assure you, sir, both have been entirely unnecessary this evening. There is no danger to be found here. Mr. Darcy is perfectly safe."

Before either man could so much as blink, she had turned—a whirling dervish of dark silk, pale skin, and raven locks as she strode across the room and out of the door.

In that moment, Darcy wanted nothing more than to turn on his heels and follow her, to soothe and console her, and to contradict her preposterous presumption, for he knew perfectly well that, so long as he remained in her vicinity, she was far from safe with him.

But she was not the only one in harm's way, for Darcy had known for some time that he was in very great danger himself: in danger of falling completely and irrevocably in love with her; but propriety—and a drawing room full of people, including Elizabeth's father—kept his feet rooted to the floor.

Propriety, propriety… Damn propriety!

Darcy silently cursed himself. So far propriety had afforded him nothing but vexation, discontent, and misfortune. His frustration and anger—at Mr. Bennet; at his own intolerable situation and his utter uselessness to Elizabeth—peaked. If anyone deserved to be reprimanded for impropriety, it certainly wasn't the slip-of-a-woman who'd managed to turn his entire world upside down in a mere handful of weeks.

Elizabeth had conducted herself with decorum during every single encounter they'd ever shared, and Darcy respected and esteemed her highly; but the thoughts and desires she unwittingly provoked in him were another matter entirely. Although he'd never voiced or acted upon them—nor would he ever, he knew, unless she willingly gave her consent to be his—he could not deny that his powerful inclinations toward her were…ungentlemanly, to say the least. His intentions, however, remained nothing but honourable.

Throughout the course of his lifetime Darcy had felt passionately about many things, but that passion was always tempered by an equally strong desire to remain in staunch control of his emotions; to think, and speak, and act in a rational manner at all times and in every circumstance. As a child, self-control was something he'd taken great pains to master; something repeatedly insisted upon and ingrained in him by his parents. Self-control was something the master of Pemberley prided himself on and possessed in abundance—prior to setting foot in Hertfordshire, that is.

Seemingly without ceremony Elizabeth Bennet had captured his notice, claimed his heart, and caused his inherently passionate nature to flare hotter than a bonfire. With each passing day, whether Darcy had the pleasure of her company or not, she'd managed to make his careful self-control wane to a disturbing degree. Some might even call it perilously close to non-existent. At times it was all he could do to keep his head on his shoulders and his ardency for her in check.

The unwelcome sound of Mr. Bennet clearing his throat returned him to the present. While Darcy could hardly fault any father for being vigilant with his children, he felt Mr. Bennet's circumspection was, in this instance, severely misplaced. The man had mortified, demeaned, and injured one of his few truly respectable daughters when his efforts would have been far better employed endeavouring to prevent his youngest two—and occasionally his wife—from flirting so shamelessly with the officers.

With a dark countenance he turned toward Mr. Bennet. Though determined to remain respectful for Elizabeth's sake, as well as his own, Darcy found it difficult to speak without using the authoritative tone he often employed as Pemberley's master.

"Mr. Bennet, with all due respect," he began, but was instantly silenced by the menacing look on the elder man's face.

"You, Mr. Darcy," he hissed, "have been playing a very dangerous game, one that you are shockingly ill-equipped to win. I strongly urge you to keep to your own kind, sir, and give my second daughter a wide berth. She is my favorite and, though it pains me exceedingly to deny her anything that affords her even the slightest measure of happiness, I will endeavour to protect her at all costs and in any manner I see fit. However honourable your intentions toward her are, take heed when I assure you that any romantic designs you have on Elizabeth will bring upon you retribution of the acutest kind."

Three

A fortnight had passed since he'd last seen her—the arch of her brow, the curve of her cheek, the graceful column of her neck. Fourteen days since he'd heard her melodic laughter, watched her lips curl into a smile, or listened to her speak the syllables of his surname.

Day after day Darcy told himself that Elizabeth's absence from society was no cause for concern, but night after night the ache in his breast—the sheer longing he felt to be in her company—only worsened. Nothing eased his hunger for her presence or quenched his thirst to hear her voice. Nothing purged her image from his mind or dulled his intense desire to know her infinitely better than he already felt he did.

What was this hold she had over him? What sort of spell had she cast with her artless beauty and engaging conversation, her fine eyes and clever wit? How many mornings had he awakened from dreams so vivid he'd confused them with reality?

Had she truly come to him in his bedchamber, he wondered; her expression and words as tender as her touch? Each time Darcy awoke and stumbled to his door—only to find it locked—the absurdity of such a scenario seemed obvious; but why, then, did his heart pound as though it might burst from his chest? Why did his lungs burn as though he hadn't been able to draw a breath? Why were his sheets a tangled mess upon the floor, and his nightshirt sweat-soaked and twisted upon his body? For the life of him, Darcy could think of no rational explanation…at least none that made any sense.

The master of Pemberley ran shaking hands through his hair. He was a disaster. If he didn't speak to Elizabeth soon he was afraid he'd go mad. But where on earth was she? When he'd brazenly called upon her at Longbourn—on a day he knew Mr. Bennet would be absent tending to business in Town—she was nowhere to be found. Neither had she attended church, or visited the village, or called upon her neighbours and friends.

Clearly, her family was keeping her under lock and key and Darcy feared it was somehow his fault. After passing so many agreeable moments together he flatly refused to believe that Elizabeth's sentiments weren't equal to his for her. The idea was simply too painful for him to contemplate. It must be Mr. Bennet who was responsible for their separation, but Darcy could not fathom why.

Had his private thoughts and desires concerning Elizabeth been known, there was no doubt in Darcy's mind her father would have deemed them wildly inappropriate; but Mr. Bennet was no mind reader, and Darcy's conduct toward his daughter had always been that befitting a gentleman. He could think of nothing he'd either said or done that might have angered the elder gentleman to such a degree as to deny his approval; nothing, that is, except the keeping of Georgiana's secret.

That Elizabeth's father would even suspect what had transpired at Ramsgate was impossible, for no one but Darcy, Georgiana, and their cousin Fitzwilliam knew of it. Of course, one of their servants could have betrayed them, but Darcy sincerely doubted that was the case, as the servants who lived at Pemberley were fiercely loyal to his family, not to mention *their* families had proved trustworthy to the Darcys for generations. But perhaps his sister's current proclivities no longer transcended that loyalty. It was a prospect that terrified him, and Darcy suddenly felt a chill in his bones that had nothing at all to do with the weather.

The view from the drawing room window was wretched, the surrounding land and everything upon it mired by drizzle and fog as far as the eye could see. It had been this way for days, and by mid-morning Darcy had reached his wits end. He'd no patience left to extend to Bingley's sisters—Miss

Bingley and Mrs. Hurst—who sought to engage him in insipid conversation, inquiring in cloying tones after *dear Georgiana*; nor did he desire to remain any longer where he'd absolutely no chance of meeting with Elizabeth Bennet.

No doubt sensing his guest's restlessness, Bingley challenged Darcy to a game of billiards, but Darcy declined and called for his greatcoat and hat instead, intent on riding out despite the miserable weather.

"Are you completely mad?" Netherfield's master cried, rising from his chair by the fire to gape incredulously at his friend. "The fog is thicker than Cook's pea soup. You'll lose your way within ten minutes and take a chill. Besides, we are to dine with the officers this afternoon, or have you forgotten? Whatever shall I tell Colonel Forster should you fail to attend?"

"You may tell the good colonel that if I'd remained any longer in this house without the benefit of fresh air and exercise, I could not have been held accountable for my actions."

Bingley frowned. "Honestly, Darcy, it's dreadful out there, not to mention cold. Do be sensible and stay at home. There can be nothing out there to hold your interest in such weather as this."

Darcy adjusted his leather riding gloves and claimed his crop from Bingley's butler, slicing the stale air of the drawing room with several quick flicks of his wrist. "I appreciate your concern, Bingley, but my mood is beastly. Trust me when I say that you and Colonel Forster would do well to be rid of me today."

"And I cannot help but disagree. However appalling your mood may be, I wish you'd reconsider and stay at home. At the risk of sounding like a woman, I won't be easy until you return."

Even as Darcy's lips twitched his resolve held firm. He tucked his crop neatly beneath his arm and donned his hat. "I've ridden out in far worse weather than this at Pemberley. You need not worry yourself over me. I'm quite used to a bit of rain."

By the time his horse was saddled and ready the rain had grown heavier, but Darcy mounted without giving the rapidly worsening weather a second thought. He flicked his reins and set off at a slow trot until he reached the crest of a nearby hill, where he took several deep, cleansing breaths. The air there was crisp and cold and helped clear some of the fog in his head, just as his journey to higher ground had led him above the fog below. With renewed focus he dug his heels into his horse's sides, urging him onward at a punishing pace, intent on exorcising his demons, or at the very least resolved to give them a good, hard run for their money.

He knew not how long he rode, nor how far, when his mount became spooked by some unseen apparition and reared. Darcy held fast to the reins, determined to keep his seat, and after some effort managed to get the stallion under control.

His exhalation as he dismounted was harsh. After cinching the reins tightly, Darcy stroked the animal's thick neck, murmuring words of assuagement. They did little to soothe man or beast, however, and Darcy squinted into the pouring rain, wondering whether there was real danger afoot. For the most part he was on open road, but the road was unfamiliar, flanked by several meters of hay with thick woods bordering either side. The trees within appeared dense and overgrown, littered with briars and dead brush; a veritable fortress that Darcy speculated could not be easily penetrated by humans unless they wielded torches, pitchforks, and sickles.

A loud crack of thunder sounded, resonating through the countryside, shaking the very ground beneath his feet. Lightening followed swiftly on its heels—several great, blinding flashes that set the leaden sky ablaze. Darcy's horse tossed his head with a terrified squeal, nostrils flared and eyes wide as the freezing rain assaulted them with renewed determination.

For one wild moment, out of the corner of his eye Darcy imagined he saw an all-too-familiar set of eyes watching him intently from between the trees, as bewitching and dark as ever—as dark as the surrounding woods. But rather than lips the colour of pale rose petals on her beloved face, these lips were dyed a deep crimson; bright, and slick, and wet.

A shock of fear shot through his breast before he realized the absurdity of such a thing and shook his head, irritated and angry with himself. *At last,* he thought darkly, *the madness has set in.* Grabbing hold of his horse's mane, Darcy jammed his foot into the stirrup and mounted, more than willing to return to the warmth of Netherfield and the devil he knew.

Four

In his absence, Jane Bennet had been invited to dine with Bingley's sisters, a change in events that made Darcy dearly wish he'd heeded Bingley's counsel and supped with the officers instead of galloping across the countryside in the midst of an electrical storm.

Evening had fallen over Hertfordshire, and yet the rain continued unabated, pelting the windows and pounding against the roof with a vengeance. As Darcy was safely ensconced in Netherfield's drawing room with a cup of hot tea in his hand, he ought to have been comfortable; but rather than enjoying the warmth of the roaring fire in the grate he was beginning to suffer the effects of a cold and was in no mood to put on pleasant airs for anyone, especially Caroline Bingley and her vapid sister.

Not that Miss Bennet was fit for company herself at the moment. Her father, ever-vigilant and intent upon going to great lengths to protect his second daughter from Darcy's attentions, had foolishly allowed his first to ride to Netherfield unaccompanied on horseback. To everyone's horror she'd arrived nearly an hour later than expected— soaking wet and chilled to the bone—and had promptly fallen ill during the first course. She was currently lodged in a guest room above stairs with a headache, a sore throat, and a slight fever. While her condition was hardly favourable, at the moment Darcy felt his was little better. Though he wasn't half as ill as Jane Bennet, Bingley had yet to return from Meryton, leaving him to pass the evening alone with Miss Bingley and Mrs. Hurst.

"Tell me, Mr. Darcy," Miss Bingley inquired as she laid aside her cards and proceeded to take a turn about the room, "why is it that you and my brother feel the need to bother with the Bennets? In my opinion, they possess nothing out of the ordinary; no superior qualities or talents to set them apart or distinguish them from the rest of their sex, unless, of course, you count the two youngest girls' appetite for officers and Eliza's penchant for scampering about the countryside. Jane Bennet, I grant you, is a sweet girl. It's a shame her connexions are so low, otherwise, I wouldn't mind knowing her better."

Mrs. Hurst hummed her agreement from the card table, abandoning her own cards to rearrange the elegant gold bangles upon her wrists.

Darcy closed his eyes and exhaled slowly. He was in no frame of mind to tolerate Caroline Bingley's jealousy, yet, out of respect for Bingley, knew he must remain civil. He took a sip of tea, wincing as he swallowed, and cleared his throat.

"I cannot deny that the youngest girls lack decorum as well as restraint," he said, "but whether they ought to be held accountable for their poor comportment when their father takes little interest in their education and upbringing, I cannot say.

"As for Miss Elizabeth Bennet, perhaps there are some amongst our general acquaintance who would consider it unconventional for a young lady to spend so much time out-of-doors, but I fail to see the harm in it; quite the opposite. I daresay her eyes are often brightened by the exercise."

An insincere smile graced Miss Bingley's countenance. "You will no doubt be interested to hear then, that Mr. Bennet has finally seen fit to exert his authority in some respect, although, regrettably, it doesn't appear to extend so far as his youngest daughters, who, in my opinion, would benefit from a healthy dose of high-handedness. But that, I suppose, is of little matter."

Darcy pursed his lips. "And you perceived such information to be of interest to me in what way, madam?"

"Come, Mr. Darcy. All of Hertfordshire has surely noticed the blatant manner in which Miss Eliza has all but thrown herself in your way. It's no wonder Mr. Bennet has forbidden her to appear before company of late. Her comportment is shameful, and rumor has it that until she is capable of conducting herself in a manner befitting a proper lady her father is to keep her locked away at home.

Apparently," she sniffed, "her continued absence from society speaks for itself."

The beginning of a headache was making his temples throb. Darcy took another sip of tea, growing impatient and annoyed. *Blatantly throwing herself in my way,* he growled inwardly. Not only was such an accusation untrue, but entirely laughable, especially considering the source. Miss Bingley had been trying to ingratiate herself with him for years with the hope of gaining his interest, and failing spectacularly with each attempt. *Good Lord. How much longer must I endure Caroline Bingley's cattiness?* Darcy wondered exasperatedly. *Would that I was above stairs in the comfort of my own apartment and free from such pettiness and vitriol—or, better yet, at Pemberley.*

When he failed to comment, Miss Bingley continued in the same vein. "What say you, Mr. Darcy? Surely, you must have an opinion on the subject. I daresay you wouldn't approve of your sister behaving in such a manner as would require her to be confined to Pemberley House, hidden away like a pariah from visitors and acquaintances whenever they came to call."

Darcy's annoyance turned to anger then as he thought of Georgiana, who was indeed at that moment in a very similar situation, residing alone in their ancestral home with no one but Colonel Fitzwilliam and the servants for company.

"Certainly, not," he replied curtly.

"Poor Eliza Bennet," Miss Bingley lamented. "But with such a mother, not to mention relations in Cheapside who no doubt live within sight of their warehouses, I can hardly say I'm surprised she turned out so headstrong and wild. I wonder if we shall ever see her again? Do you think, Louisa, she will be let out before Christmas? I daresay it will hardly matter at that point, as we will more than likely be safely removed to Grosvenor Street by then."

While both sisters cackled delightedly, Darcy stewed in silence until their unconscionable tittering became too much and he found he could no longer hold his temper in check.

"I wouldn't put much stock in second-hand gossip, madam, if I were you, for there is rarely much truth to be found in blind assumptions. Should you assume wrongly, your misfortunes would be heavy indeed."

A frown appeared on Miss Bingely's face. "Oh? How so, sir?"

With pursed lips, Darcy placed his cup and saucer on a nearby table with more force than he'd intended and rose from his chair, crossing the room in several long strides to stand before her. "To assume wrongly, Miss Bingley," he said lowly, "you would succeed only in casting yourself in a most unpropitious and unflattering light, especially since all of Hertfordshire must certainly have noticed the fervency of my admiration of the very lady you are so intent on disparaging. In fact, it's been many weeks now that I've considered Miss Elizabeth Bennet one of the handsomest women of my acquaintance."

The lady's eyes widened in shock, and for once she appeared to have nothing to say.

Darcy's satisfaction at having rendered her speechless was short-lived, however, as he recalled he was not only a guest in Bingley's home, but in Miss Bingley's as well, and a gentleman—not some indecorous churl. Clearly, the time had come for him to take his leave and withdraw above stairs for the rest of the night. "Pray excuse me," he muttered as he offered both women a stiff, conciliatory bow. "I'm afraid I'm feeling unwell, and will retire to my apartment directly. Good evening to you."

Five

Wide bands of sunlight shone through the bedchamber windows, eliciting a low groan from Darcy as he shielded his eyes with his hands. The stark brightness made the pounding in his head unbearable, and he cursed whatever servant was responsible for daring to draw the curtains that morning without first obtaining his consent. Throughout the night the master of Pemberley's repose had been fitful at best, and now, in addition to a throbbing headache, he suffered a sore throat, chills, and a fever.

Parched with thirst, Darcy licked his lips and squinted toward the bedside table, hoping to discover a pitcher of water. He struggled to sit upright and was nearly overcome by the effort it cost him. The encroaching blackness behind his eyes and ringing in his ears made his head spin, and for several excruciating moments he fought against the urge to retch.

Swallowing thickly, he wiped beads of sweat from his brow with shaking fingers and willed the sensation to pass. He'd no recollection of ever feeling so weak and helpless, even as a young boy. As a grown man, enduring such a situation was nothing short of intolerable, yet here he was, powerless and without a remedy in sight.

With a muttered exhalation he felt for the bell pull, yanked the cord, and collapsed onto his pillow, where he prayed that his man Jennings would soon appear with an elixir that would magically restore him to health. As unlikely as it was, at the moment it was all the hope Darcy had.

Darcy was having the strangest dream. Elizabeth Bennet was standing in his bedchamber wearing nothing but a dressing gown the color of fresh cream. A riotous mess of curls framed her face and tumbled down her back, giving her the appearance of a nighttime fey, untamed and otherworldly as she argued quietly with his valet from the foot of his bed.

"I should not be here," she insisted, her eyes darting to where Darcy lay, then away. "It was very wrong of me to come."

In her hand she held a taper made of beeswax. Its flame bathed her features in glowing warmth, rendering her so beautiful that Darcy suddenly found it difficult to breathe. How long had it been since he'd seen her? How long since he'd inhaled her sweet scent? At the moment he couldn't recall. He knew only that he'd missed her beyond reason, that he craved her presence more than food or water, exercise and air.

"You mustn't speak so," Jennings chided. "Not when you may be of help."

Elizabeth shook her head. "I'm not a doctor. Though I wish it with all my heart, I can do nothing for Mr. Darcy that would not result in more pain and a lifetime of regret, for both of us. You'd do far better to send for Mr. Jones."

Jennings scoffed. "Mr. Jones intends to bleed him unless he is better by morning. Cutting into his flesh will only rob my master of what little energy he has left. I cannot allow it, not when it is within your power to offer him far more than any local butcher-turned-apothecary. In fact, after seeing you standing here as you live and breathe, I'm willing to bet my life on it."

Elizabeth turned aside her head. "Then you are delusional. Human life is not something to be bartered, but revered; cherished and protected at all costs. Nothing should be allowed to taint or poison it."

"And so long as you are here, my dear lady, I have no doubt it shall be so, which is why I implore you—out of the goodness of your heart—to help my master. Indeed, you must."

"Indeed, I *cannot.* If it was within my power to do so, I swear to you I would, but I have no such ability. As I told you before, I am no surgeon. In fact, I am—in every way—exactly the opposite of what your master requires. It pains me to say it, but Mr. Darcy's recovery must be left to Mr. Jones. I can only pray it will be enough."

Jennings, however, would hear none of it and, with a steely glint of determination, said forcefully, "It will certainly *not* be enough, Miss Bennet, not by any means!

"I've known Mr. Darcy since he was a boy. My loyalty and affection for him—for the entire Darcy family—is deeply rooted, as was my father's and his father's before him. I cannot simply stand by and do nothing for my master when his life is at stake, not when I know of a way to help.

"Miss Bennet," he said earnestly, "the general concurrence is that Mr. Darcy is highly unlikely to overcome this illness without intervention; therefore, certain concessions will have to be made immediately. I'm willing to accept full responsibility for any and all consequences incurred by those concessions, no matter their nature. *When* you save him—for there is no other option before us—I will continue to guard your secrets and those of your family as closely as I have my master's. I swear it."

Elizabeth shook her head. "I have no secrets," she began indignantly, but Jennings silenced her with one hard look.

"Unlike your neighbours, I am neither ignorant, nor blind. I know what you are, just as I know precisely what is and is not within your power."

The silence that followed was neither easy, nor comfortable, but thick and suffocating; charged, as though the entire room and everything in it might implode at any moment. Darcy's heavy-lidded gaze flickered between Jennings and Elizabeth with increasing unease, a growing sense of urgency mounting in his breast.

Then, before his eyes, Elizabeth underwent a shocking metamorphosis that made his blood run cold. No longer was she the delightful, teasing young woman he admired so ardently, but a foreign, esoteric creature whose entire presence radiated acute and immediate danger.

There was something disturbingly familiar about the dark glint in her eyes, though; the slow curl of her mouth; the way she moved—methodically, determinedly, with an ethereal grace that chilled him to the bone. Her slender body seemed to glide toward Jennings as her candle cast heavy, distorted shadows on the bedchamber walls and all that lay within.

"You presume a great deal, then," she hissed, her voice uncharacteristically menacing, "and it is because you presume a great deal that I must caution you to keep your presumptions to yourself from this moment forward, or you may find yourself in a dangerous predicament from which *you* will never recover!"

Despite the sinister image Elizabeth presented, Jennings did not shrink from her, but stood his ground, meeting her baleful stare with every appearance of composure and no hint of fear. "In my opinion, madam, the only person in this room currently facing a dangerous predicament from which he may never recover is my poor master.

"As for your other charges, I am Mr. Darcy's valet. While it isn't my place to presume anything about anyone, as his oldest and most trusted servant it *is* my duty to make observations, especially pertaining to my master and all that affects him.

"For instance," he continued lowly, "since you've come to Netherfield to attend your ailing sister, you've made countless inquiries about my master and his health. As your agitation and concern for him appeared sincere and heartfelt, I concluded that you must care for Mr. Darcy. The fact that you're standing here now, in his private apartment in the middle of the night and at very great risk, not only to your own reputation, but to that of your family as well, confirms it.

"You might also be interested to know, Miss Bennet, that you just so happen to share several...let us say...*unique* physical traits with a certain young lady of my master's intimate acquaintance. Miss Darcy would be inconsolable if her beloved elder brother were to succumb to an ailment so trifling as a fever when she, or someone very much like her, could easily have prevented it."

Elizabeth, who only seconds before had been glaring so malevolently at Jennings, furrowed her brows in confusion at such a curious statement. A moment later, however, her hands all but flew to her mouth, muffling her gasp of horror. "No," she said on a breath, her eyes wide with alarm, "*that* can't be possible…"

But Jennings neither confirmed, nor denied his implication. He simply continued to look Elizabeth steadily in the eye and said firmly, "We are wasting precious time, Miss Bennet. Nothing Mr. Jones administered thus far has yielded any improvement, nor is it likely that anything he attempts on the morrow will provide a satisfactory outcome. It is too late at this point to send to London for a physician. If Mr. Darcy's fever doesn't break soon your apothecary bleeding him will be the least of our worries. To put it bluntly, he will die."

Elizabeth swallowed thickly and closed her eyes. "And what is it you will have me do?" she whispered harshly. "My hands are tied just as tightly as yours! What can be done? I know very well there is nothing within reason—nothing within the laws of nature—that can be done!"

"I'm afraid desperate times call for desperate measures. Fortunately, I happen to have knowledge of several unique options before us that could be most effective in restoring Mr. Darcy to health."

Elizabeth opened her eyes. Jennings removed his handkerchief from his waistcoat pocket and offered it to her. She accepted it, averted her gaze, and dabbed at the moisture on her cheeks. "Thank you," she murmured.

The valet merely inclined his head and indicated two comfortable looking chairs by the hearth. "Come, Miss Bennet, and I will tell you of my plan. For my master's sake we cannot afford to tarry any longer. Of course, we must try the less drastic of the two measures first, before attempting the other, infinitely more…unalterable solution, but I have every confidence Mr. Darcy will soon be himself again, no matter what method we must employ."

Six

When Darcy awakened it was nearly dawn. His body was no longer ravaged by fever, but soothed by slender fingers and a pliant form. Every touch bestowed upon him was gentle, lingering, and undeniably affectionate. Each caressing pass over his body radiated incomparable heat that seared his skin and warmed him from within, despite the surprisingly icy temperature of her flesh. Darcy drew a shuddering breath, inhaled her sweetness, and silently prayed the young woman draped across his chest was indeed real and not merely a figment of his over-active imagination. Pressing his lips to the top of her head, he acted upon impulse and encircled her in his arms, holding her as he'd so often desired, but never truly believed to be possible.

"Mr. Darcy?" she whispered, lifting her head from his shoulder with a start to look upon him, concern and relief apparent in her eyes.

He sighed with contentment and wound his fingers into her hair, cradling the back of her head and easing her closer until their foreheads nearly touched. "Elizabeth," he rasped, his voice hoarse after heaven-knows how many days without use. "Thank God you're here."

"Yes," she murmured with feeling. "Thank God. Thank God you are out of danger."

Her breath was ambrosia against his lips, and Darcy desperately wanted to taste her; to capture her mouth with his in a tender, heartfelt kiss. "Elizabeth," he repeated on a breath, his eyes intent upon her lips.

He watched in fascination as the tip of her tongue appeared, moistening her bottom lip before disappearing once more. "I am here, dear sir."

Before Darcy could act, however, the sound of a throat being discreetly cleared was heard and Jennings emerged from the sitting room, a hint of amusement in his expression as he addressed his master warmly. "You certainly had us worried, sir. Did he not, Miss Bennet?"

Elizabeth nodded once, a curt inclination of her head, before expelling a tremulous breath and slowly withdrawing from Darcy's embrace.

Already the master of Pemberley missed the comfort of her touch more than he could say—more than he could even fathom—and was on the verge of commanding her to return to him when the impropriety of their situation suddenly hit him with the force of a runaway carriage. Shocked, Darcy gaped at her, his words catching in his throat as he watched Elizabeth silently lift the counterpane and slip from his bed, hurriedly smoothing the creases in her dressing gown with unsteady fingers. To his dismay, he realized it was the same gown he'd envisioned her wearing in his dream the previous night.

Good God, what a dream it was—so strange and disturbing. Darcy frowned. At least, it had certainly felt like a dream to him at the time…

Darcy's inhalation was swift and sharp, and brought on a coughing fit that wracked his body.

Ever efficient, Jennings procured a glass of water and assisted his master to drink while Elizabeth hovered at his bedside, her expression deeply troubled as Darcy's coughing slowly abated. He dropped his head back onto the pillows and closed his eyes, his head spinning as the missing pieces settled into place.

Last night had been no fever-induced dream! Elizabeth Bennet had indeed come to his bedchamber—at the behest of his valet, no less—and lain with him in his bed. At one point Jennings had argued with her and brashly accused her of being something unthinkable: he'd accused her of being like Georgiana.

Impossible," Darcy whispered raggedly, pressing the heels of his hands against his eyes. *Impossible!* There was no way Elizabeth, so perfect and pure of heart, could possibly be such an unspeakable creature anymore than his most trusted servant could have suggested such an abhorrent thing to her in the first place.

But the image of his fifteen-year-old sister immediately came to mind and gave him reason to pause. It was true. Georgiana was indeed a vampyre, but she was still essentially the same sweet, kind-hearted, inherently good girl she had always been. She still loved music—Bach and Beethoven—and played her pianoforte as beautifully as she ever had. Of course, her more recent proclivities had presented a bit of a challenge initially, most of her focus being on her music master and the pulsing artery beneath his cravat than the new sheet music he'd brought with him from Vienna. Fortunately, Darcy and Fitzwilliam were able to usher her out of the music room before she could give herself away, or—God forbid—inflict any damage upon the poor, unsuspecting gentleman.

Darcy shuddered at the remembrance and chanced a look at Elizabeth, who regarded him cautiously, her bottom lip caught between her teeth. His heart pounded against his ribs as he studied her beloved face—her dark eyes, her snow-white skin, her pale lips. All the signs were there, staring steadily back at him, leaving him in no doubt of the truth. He wondered why on earth he'd never made the connection before. Impulsively, he reached out and took her hand in his. It was as he'd suspected. Her fingers were freezing; colder than ice—nay, as cold as death itself.

Elizabeth's expression was nothing short of terrified as she attempted to snatch her hand away, but Darcy held fast to her, refusing to release her so easily. To his surprise, Elizabeth relented and allowed it.

"Jennings," he muttered darkly, his eyes fixed upon the woman before him as he struggled to regain his composure. "I shall deal with you later. Right now I desire a private audience with Miss Bennet."

"Your hands, madam," Darcy said as he looked pointedly into her eyes, "are freezing. You must warm yourself by the fire before you catch your death."

Elizabeth released a tremulous breath. "I believe we both know a fire will do little to warm me. As for catching my death, it is kind of you to worry, but you should concern yourself with your own health. There is very little you, or anyone else, can do about the state of mine." She bowed her head. "I feel deeply for your dear sister, though. To become…what she is, and at so young an age, cannot be a happy thing for either of you."

"Indeed," he muttered. The physical distance between them was far closer than what was considered proper in any circumstance, but at the moment even a few inches seemed too great a divide, even after such a startling revelation. Darcy tugged firmly on her hand, effectively pulling her onto the bed to sit beside him. After all was said and done, the fact that Elizabeth was a vampyre inspired no fear or abhorrence in him, but the outrage he felt on her behalf for the atrocities he imagined she'd endured before and during her transformation was another matter.

Though he'd watched, alarmed as she threatened his only-too-human valet the night before, seeing her as she was now—her gaze soft, almost sorrowful—only confirmed what Darcy had always believed in his heart: that it wasn't in Elizabeth's nature to willfully inflict harm on anyone for any reason, least of all someone for whom she cared. In fact, she'd not only listened to Jennings, but allowed him to persuade her to nurse Darcy back to health in a most unconventional and improper manner, and at great personal risk—not only to her reputation, but to her family's as well. Darcy knew no one so generous, or so good, save perhaps for Georgiana. Yes. The woman at his side was still his Elizabeth in every way that mattered. To Darcy, she could never—*would* never—be anything else.

Elizabeth spoke then, and the softness of her voice soothed him, even though her words had the opposite effect. "May I inquire as to how your sister became…like me?"

Unconsciously, Darcy tightened his grip on her hand. It was a story he'd much rather forget, but for Elizabeth he'd do anything, even relive the most painful day of his life.

"She was taken from school," he began, "to Ramsgate, where an establishment was procured for her. Her companion, a Mrs. Young, in whose character we were grievously deceived, resided there with her. Rather than act as chaperone to Georgiana, she neglected her and carelessly granted her liberties she should not have been permitted, such as walking to the seaside without so much as a maid to accompany her. One day, while wandering through the village, Georgiana was approached by a man. She was then but fifteen."

Darcy shut his eyes, his pain as fresh as the day he'd arrived and discovered them. "I believe his main object was her dowry of £30,000, and that in order to obtain it he intended to seduce her, then convince her to elope with him; but, unwilling to grieve a brother more than ten years her senior, Georgiana wrote to me and I joined them unexpectedly, before he'd been able to succeed with his seduction or obtain her consent.

"I'd spoilt his carefully laid plans, and his anger and resentment was such that he meant to punish me for my interference by killing her. He told me so just before he sank his teeth into her neck. By the grace of God, I was able to tear her away from him before he could do his worst. His bite was not fatal and any injuries she'd sustained were healed during her transformation.

"I need not tell you the life Georgiana leads now is not the life she knew before. She was spared from true death, only to be condemned to another fate no less grievous, and every bit as final."

"Does the hateful one who bit Miss Darcy still walk this earth?" she asked.

"No. My cousin Richard, with whom I share guardianship of Georgiana, is a colonel in Her Majesty's Army. He aided me in my revenge. The villain may be no more, but my sweet, innocent sister must forever suffer his curse."

"I am sorry for all of you," Elizabeth whispered feelingly. "It is a dreadful infliction; one I would not wish upon my worst enemy, never mind one as undeserving of such unsolicited horror as your young sister undoubtedly was."

Darcy merely inclined his head. "And what of you, Miss Bennet?" he asked sedately. "How is it that you have come to be in a similar state as my sister?"

"Oh no," she responded with a frown. "I'm afraid the story of my immortality isn't half as sinister as poor Miss Darcy's. As a matter of fact, it's rather insignificant in comparison."

"Nothing about you is insignificant, but if speaking of it distresses you, then you need not relate the particulars to me. In fact, I will never ask you again."

The barest hint of a smile tugged at her lips. "You flatter me, Mr. Darcy," she said, taking a deep breath as she tucked a long, glossy curl behind her ear. "Very well. As you might already know, my father's estate is entailed away from the female line, requiring him to sire a son to succeed him and to ensure my mother and any unmarried children may remain at Longbourn after his death. Since he and my mother failed to produce a male heir, Longbourn will pass to a distant cousin in Kent.

"Though we are comfortable, we are hardly rich. My sisters and I have no dowries to speak of, so my father, in his desperation to provide for us, traveled several years ago to the darkest corner of London. He'd heard mention of a gentleman who, for a price, would assist him in taking very specific measures to ensure he'd remain master of Longbourn, always."

Darcy could hardly credit what he was hearing. "You cannot mean…" he whispered, horror-struck at the lengths to which Mr. Bennet would go in order to keep his legacy within his family.

Elizabeth turned aside her head. "Yes," she quietly confirmed. "My father shall live forever, and I am to be his companion."

Seven

"What of your mother and sisters?" Darcy inquired. He'd always thought Elizabeth favoured her father while her sisters resembled their mother, but it was now evident that Mr. Bennet's second daughter had far more in common with her father than mere physical appearance.

Elizabeth shook her head. "They are human, though Jane knows precisely what we are and why. She has kept our secret and always shall, but I fear it's been very hard on her. She is constantly worried for us, as you must also worry for your sister."

"Of course," he agreed absently, running his hand over his mouth, deep in thought. While he could relate to Mr. Bennet's desire—and even his desperation—to provide for his family using whatever means were within his grasp, after seeing Georgiana through the agony of her transformation and the harried, emotional months that followed, the master of Pemberley disagreed with the elder man's solution, especially when Mr. Bennet's decision ultimately sentenced Elizabeth, a favourite child, to such a difficult and dangerous existence.

"Your father made a conscious choice, did he not, to become what he is?" he asked.

"He did. Though I've often questioned his sanity, I've never questioned his devotion. He cares for us, and paid the ultimate price in order to assure our future at Longbourn."

Darcy resisted the urge to snort derisively. In his opinion, Mr. Bennet would have done far better to save and invest his income so his wife could purchase another home after his demise, or grow their daughters' meager dowries, but that was a moot point at this juncture. The damage done was tragic and irreversible for all parties, whether some were aware of the sacrifices made or not.

The master of Pemberley struggled to keep his temper in check and exhaled roughly. "Your father had no right to contemplate such an act of selfish defiance, never mind commit one. He'd no right to condemn you to a fate no sane person would *ever* choose for himself or his family. Forgive me, but if he desired a companion he ought to have bestowed such an honour upon your mother, yet he did not. He forced it upon you instead."

To his surprise, a wry smile tugged at her lips. "You've been in company with my mother on many occasions, sir. As dear as she is to me, the soul of discretion she is not; nor does she practice economy, or exercise restraint of any kind. I fear she'd make a poor vampyre."

"You can joke about such a thing?" he asked, his tone incredulous.

"I must," was her matter-of-fact reply, "or else the regret—the knowledge that I'll never have a husband, or children—would consume me. I believe you are well enough acquainted with me to know I wasn't formed for melancholy. I've simply chosen to carry on as though nothing has changed. Trust me when I say it's far better this way, for all of us."

Darcy pursed his lips, furious that she'd had so much taken from her, and all because her father was both foolhardy and self-serving enough to devise and carry out such a damning subterfuge!

As though she'd sensed the bent of his thoughts, Elizabeth placed her hand upon his arm and shook her head sadly. "My father may have chosen this path for himself, but he certainly didn't choose to make me his image on a whim. You must believe me when I tell you it was out of necessity; nothing more, nothing less."

"There can be no necessity so urgent as to sentence one's own child to such a fate," he replied harshly. "No truly loving parent would ever resort to such an *option*."

"Mr. Darcy, tell me you would simply do nothing if your daughter lay dying. Tell me, if you had the means to save her—the child you cherished most in the world—you would choose differently. After being thrown from my horse three years ago, my injuries were so severe there was no hope for recovery. I was also in great pain, which in turn pained my family."

For a long moment he regarded her in silence, his eyes taking in every detail of her person, searching for any sign of former injury; but, as with Georgiana, he could see no blemish, could detect no flaw. He lowered his eyes. "Would you have returned the favour last night? Would you have acted similarly yourself if the chill of your body failed to drive the fever from my own?"

Elizabeth swallowed thickly and looked away. "We were not speaking of you and I, but of my father and myself."

"That's true," he conceded, "but you must understand—by now you must know it's *you* who I've come to cherish more than any other, yet I cannot imagine making the same choice in such a case without first obtaining your consent."

"Then it appears we are of one mind," she responded heatedly, "but know this, sir: if I were to ever again find myself faced with the prospect of your imminent death—of poor Miss Darcy being left entirely alone in the world to shift for herself—I would be forced to consider it, and perhaps even act upon it, but only as a last resort. This is not an easy existence, Mr. Darcy, as you and your sister are well aware. Unless your need last night was not most dire, I never would have wanted you to know it."

He shook his head emphatically. "But I *do* know it. I knew it before through Georgiana, and now, because of you. As you can see, there's little point in trying to protect me, my dear. It's far too late for that."

An affectionate smile tugged at the corners of his mouth as he imagined the two women he loved most in the world—Elizabeth and Georgiana—together at Pemberley. The prospect of the two someday becoming sisters pleased Darcy beyond measure, and he was suddenly impatient, not only to give voice to his fantasy, but to make that fantasy a reality.

"You will do her a world of good, you know. Your friendship, along with your inherent kindness and affectionate nature, will bring Georgiana unparalleled joy." He brought her hands to his lips and kissed them reverently. "You can offer her so much, Elizabeth, and I have no doubt it will be your guidance and perseverance that will enable my sister to forge her own path to happiness and contentment. She'll admire and love you straight away; in time, perhaps even as much as I do."

Elizabeth tugged her hands from his grasp and rose from the bed. Darcy stared at her, startled and disconcerted by her sudden withdrawal.

"I would be honoured to be a friend to Miss Darcy, sir, as I am honoured to be yours, but to more than that I cannot consent."

Darcy felt the colour drain from his face. "I was under the impression that our fellowship had transcended the bonds of mere friendship some time ago. Surely, after everything we confided in each other tonight—after the astounding intimacy we've shared—you can be in no doubt of my intentions toward you."

"Mr. Darcy, pray do not—"

"No, Miss Bennet," he said thickly. "I must, indeed I must. I love you, most ardently, and I beg you to end my suffering and consent to be my wife."

Elizabeth shut her eyes tightly and covered her mouth with her hand.

"Elizabeth," he said gently, and extended his hand to her. "Come here, dear heart." But Elizabeth remained where she was, silent and still as she struggled to keep her composure.

When she finally found her voice, it was solemn and subdued, rather than emotive and warm, and Darcy's heart sank as he listened to her say, "As flattered and moved as I am by your declaration, Mr. Darcy, and, despite the fervency of my own feelings regarding the matter, I must ask you to never speak such words to me again. You must surely know, dear sir, no matter how much I desire it, that I can never consent to become your wife."

*E*ight

In shock he stared at her, unable to completely credit what he'd heard. "Why ever not?" he demanded, his voice harsher than he'd intended.

Elizabeth blinked back tears. "You know very well why not."

"No. I possess no such answer. I see nothing wrong with wanting to have a life with you; nothing wrong with wanting to make you my wife. I'm in love with you for God's sake, and judging by your actions throughout the entirety of our acquaintance, I'm certain you care deeply for me as well. Does that count for nothing?"

"It's true," she conceded. "I do love you, but what you're asking of me is not only unrealistic, but dangerous! *You* are a man, *I* am a monster," she said fiercely, swiping at the moisture upon her cheeks, "and that makes any connection between us not only reprehensible, but unspeakable. A union between us would be considered an abomination in every respect, so pray do not make this any more difficult than it already is by speaking of impossibilities."

"But it need not be so," he countered. "No one beyond you and I would ever know. My household staff is loyal and trustworthy, the very soul of discretion. Your secret will be as well guarded at Pemberley as it is at Longbourn."

"My father will know. Miss Darcy and Jane will know, and I daresay none of them would approve, and rightly so. I'm no longer *human*. My body will never be able to receive yours the way a wife is meant to receive her husband. The risk to your life is far too great. I'll never be able to give you children, or warm your bed on a cold night. My flesh will always feel like ice to your touch. Should I ever forget myself in a moment of ardency, my kisses could cause your *death*. I may be innocent, Mr. Darcy, but I'm not so naïve as to believe *any* man would desire to share his marital bed with a corpse any more than he'd desire to become one himself."

Darcy clenched his jaw. The illicit references Elizabeth made to husbands and wives and marital beds agitated the master of Pemberley every bit as much as did her bitterness and despair. He would never dream of dismissing any of her concerns, for they were entirely real and valid, but at the moment his mind was so overrun by provocative images that he found it difficult to focus on anything other than the prospect of tasting her lips as they shared a searing kiss, his hands on her body as he loved her in his bed, and her back arching in pleasure as he made her his in every possible way.

Flushed with desire, he held her dark gaze until she finally lowered her eyes and turned away. Her breathing was uneven—as uneven, he noted, as his own harsh breaths. Seeing her thus did little to quell his need for her, and Darcy watched, transfixed, as she padded to the hearth and stood with her back to him. The soft glow of the fire illuminated her form from behind, affording him a scandalous glimpse of her silhouette through the translucent layers of her dressing gown and nightshift.

Darcy swallowed audibly and ran slightly shaking fingers through his hair. He'd be a complete fool to think a union between Elizabeth and he could ever be anything but dangerous. The intensity of their connection was far too powerful to be ignored. The flame of their attraction burned too bright to be extinguished by even the fiercest tempest. Surely, despite their differences, they'd be able to find some sort of common ground, though—a way to be intimate with each other physically; one that wouldn't result in his demise. *Perhaps, given time and familiarity...*Darcy mused, completely enthralled by the contour of Elizabeth's legs, the swell of her hips, and the gentle dip of her waist beneath the gossamer folds of her gown.

The mantle clock struck four, its delicate chimes resounding almost sharply in the charged silence of the room. With some effort, Darcy wrenched his eyes from Elizabeth's person and trained them instead on the window across from his bed, breathing deeply as he struggled to get his emotions in hand.

The sky, as seen through a narrow gap in the curtains, resembled a canvas of inky black; the very darkest hour before dawn. Darcy rubbed his eyes tiredly with the pads of his fingers, coughing as he exhaled roughly. His spasms subsided quickly enough, but the urge to abandon his sickbed and go to the woman across the room, wrap her in his embrace, and assure her all would somehow be well was consuming. Before he could do much more than toss the counterpane aside, however, Elizabeth was at his side, easing him back upon the pillows, reminding him of his weakened health, and urging him to lay still.

Emotionally and physically drained, Darcy allowed her ministrations without protest, his eyes trained intently upon the familiar garnet cross around her neck. It swung gently from its short chain like a pendulum as she moved over him and arranged his bedding, the firelight lending the gemstone an almost bloody richness. Entranced, he lifted his hand and stilled it, holding it in his palm.

The pendant was truly beautiful and felt smooth to his touch. Like its owner, an inexplicable sensation of warmth and comfort radiated from within it, making the polished stone seem anything but cold to him, despite the deathly temperature of Elizabeth's flesh.

Where the cross rested against the hollow of her throat, however, the master of Pemberley discerned a small, angry-looking mark that could not but concern him. Though she'd worn this particular necklace countless times before—in fact, he'd never seen her without it—his new understanding of what she was made him question her preference for it. Darcy frowned. To him, it made no sense.

"Why do you wear this?" he murmured, his fingertips caressing her injured flesh with unexampled tenderness. "Surely this causes you a great deal of discomfort?"

Elizabeth's breath hitched, and it took several moments for her to compose herself enough to form an answer. "It's a reminder of my former humanity; an admonition, so I may do the right thing when all I desire to do is wrong. When compared to the constant burn of my thirst, or the agony I would feel should I forget myself for a fraction of a moment and bring harm to someone, the discomfort is nothing—no more than an insignificant pinch. It is worth it, for it has given me the strength to spare every life I've ever wanted to take, including your own."

Darcy was shocked by her confession. She was a vampyre, after all, and undoubtedly wanted—needed—human blood in order to survive. "But I'd thought... Forgive me," he muttered, shaking his head contritely. "It must be extremely difficult abstaining from something so vital to your survival. I had no idea abstinence was even possible for those of your kind, never mind practiced."

"There are other ways for a vampyre to sustain one's self," she quietly admitted, "but that isn't to say I don't feel the urge to give in to far baser cravings whenever the options available to me appear less than palatable, which they very often do. The good Lord knows I would endure far more, though—far, far more than I ever have if only..."

"If only..." he urged softly.

But Elizabeth swallowed thickly and shook her head, shutting her eyes tightly and avoiding his gaze.

"Dearest, Elizabeth," he whispered, his voice urgent as his hands moved to cradle her face, but it was all he could manage before he felt the heady sensation of her breath envelope him. The subtle chill and deceptive sweetness of her scent made Darcy feel at once lethargic and dreamy, weightless and sublime, as though he was floating on a cloud without a care in the world.

"You must sleep now, dear sir," she whispered, her dark eyes compelling as her fingers danced along his temple, the apple of his cheek, the line of his jaw. Her hands trembled as they slid along the column of his throat, caressing his pulse and the thick, vital vein pumping his life's blood through his body with a feather-light touch. Her lips followed the same path, teasing him, pressing careful kisses to his skin as she wound her fingers into his hair.

Darcy was drowning in desire, his thoughts little more than an incoherent haze in his head. He swore he heard Elizabeth's breath quicken as she nuzzled the curve of his neck with her nose, inhaling deeply.

He felt her lips part against his throat, and the tip of her tongue trace a lazy pattern along the artery there, the sensation causing them both to moan in pleasure as his eyes rolled back into his head.

His heart pounded wildly, and he longed to know whether this experience was indeed reality or merely his subconscious deceiving him—again. But his eyelids were far too heavy to open; his limbs too burdensome to lift, and so the master of Pemberley had no option before him but to surrender to the pleasurable smother of Elizabeth's breath, and lips, and touch, unsure of everything but the fierceness of his love for her.

Nine

Pemberley, Derbyshire, two months later…

Dearest Sir,

For so very dear to me you have become. Pray forgive my forwardness in writing to you, but time is of the essence and I must speak to you by such means are within my reach. Would that our situation was not so hopeless—that our every circumstance was fated for pleasure and promise, rather than disappointment and despair—but I fear nothing can ever be so simple where you and I are concerned, and so it is with a heavy heart that I must take matters into my own hands, lest we both do something truly unforgivable.

At my father's behest, I am to leave Hertfordshire for London to stay with my aunt and uncle in Gracechurch Street. My departure is bittersweet, as the Gardiners—and my aunt especially—have long been particular favourites of mine and Jane's.

Please do not attempt to follow me there, but recall instead the many hours we have spent together as I will—fondly, and with the very deepest affection. Though we have known one another but a few precious months, your friendship has been the most important of my life. I hope with all my heart I will always have it, as you shall have mine, and much, much more.

May God bless you and keep you, and grant you every happiness. Be assured, dear sir, I will remain…

Yours, most faithfully,

E.B.

With a long exhalation Darcy laid Elizabeth's letter upon his desk and cradled his head in his hands. It certainly wasn't the first time he'd read it, or the tenth, or the five-and-tenth. For months he'd scrutinized the elegant slant of her handwriting and endeavoured to discern some deeper meaning within her words, some clue as to what his course of action ought to be; but each time he came up empty, and his questions remained unanswered.

She'd asked him not to follow her, so why had she mentioned the name of her relations, as well as her destination? Was it merely so he wouldn't worry about her? Or had she intended something more by their inclusion? For the life of him, Darcy had no idea. He knew only that he missed her beyond reason, almost beyond his sanity.

With a groan, he gripped his hair tightly with his fists. How many times in the past few months had he considered calling for his carriage and setting off for London, but saddled his fastest horse instead and rode him hard—perhaps even recklessly—until man and beast were both panting and sweating, ready to drop? How many evenings had he drunk himself into a stupor, pining for her touch in the middle of the night, her musical laughter during the day, and her incomparable presence in general? Far too many to count, he realized.

The ache in his chest was almost unbearable tonight. He exhaled again, raggedly, and clenched his jaw until his temples throbbed.

"Come now, Cousin," a familiar voice chided from the doorway. "Nothing can be as bad as your appearance implies."

Darcy raised his head with a start. Colonel Fitzwilliam was leaning against the door jamb, his arms crossed over his chest.

"I thought you and Georgiana were...out," Darcy rasped, averting his eyes as he attempted to assume some small semblance of composure, however impossible a feat it seemed at the moment.

"We went hunting earlier," the colonel replied pleasantly, "without your beloved dogs, as per your request, but Georgiana was impatient to return to her pianoforte, and so here I am."

"Good." Darcy raked his fingers through his hair and waved his hand absently toward the sideboard with a frown. "I'd offer you some brandy, Richard, but I suppose that would be pointless."

The colonel chuckled. "Entirely, though I can't say I don't miss the camaraderie attached to the gesture. It's true my tastes have…shifted, but that's neither here nor there." He patted his waistcoat pocket, where Darcy knew he carried a silver-plated flask. "I'm always well stocked these days. No need to concern yourself with me."

Darcy tried to repress his grimace and failed. "Is that so?" he inquired tightly.

"Why, of course." Fitzwilliam's demeanour turned serious as he closed the door to Darcy's study with a soft click and joined his cousin at his desk. "I would never do anything to jeopardize anyone here at Pemberley," he said sincerely, claiming the chair opposite Darcy and folding his hands upon his lap, "or any other person for that matter. It is why Georgiana and I hunt game rather than…well, *other* fare. If you'd prefer I decamp, I'll do so immediately, but—"

"No," Darcy muttered, rubbing his eyes tiredly. "No. I'm glad to have you here, Richard. You've been a world of comfort to Georgiana, and to me as well. Frankly, I wouldn't know what to do with her if you were to go away now. Considering the circumstances, it's the very least I can do for you. If you hadn't been here last autumn while I was away visiting Bingley, God knows what would have happened to her, or to the staff." He pursed his lips and shook his head angrily. "I owe you a debt I will never be able to repay."

Shortly after dawn on the morning Darcy's fever had broken, Elizabeth's father arrived at Netherfield to collect her. Her middle sister Mary accompanied him, and was instructed to reside there in Elizabeth's stead for however long she was required. Though Jane had beseeched her father to allow Elizabeth to remain to nurse her until she was recovered enough to return to Longbourn, such pleas fell on deaf ears. Elizabeth was escorted out of the house by Mr. Bennet and taken first to Longbourn, and then to Town to her uncle's house in Cheapside. She was gone from the country before the Netherfield family emerged from their bedchambers to break their fast.

Darcy's first trip below stairs came several days later and was, coincidentally, also Jane's. It was she who sought him out in the quietude of Bingley's library, she who informed him of Elizabeth's departure, and she who discreetly slipped her sister's letter into his hand while Mary sat primly across the room immersed in a thick, dusty tome. It was nothing short of torture to remain by Jane's side making polite conversation for a quarter-of-an-hour when all Darcy desired was to return to his apartment and devour the flowing script on the little piece of paper he clutched in his fist.

After reading and rereading Elizabeth's words, however, he was forced to come to terms with the fact that she wasn't going to be accessible to him for some time, either in Hertfordshire or London. Her inaccessibility didn't stop Darcy from entertaining the idea of quitting Netherfield to take up residence in Town, though, where he happened to own a house on Brooke Street.

What Darcy *wanted* to do wasn't what he knew he *ought* to do, however, which was to respect Elizabeth's request for privacy and leave her alone.

As soon as Mr. Jones pronounced him recovered enough to travel, Darcy steeled his resolve and departed for Pemberley instead. He'd been gone from his estate long enough and his impatience to see his sister, rather than read about her well-being and progress in letters from his cousin Richard, was considerable. As deeply as he longed to be reunited with Elizabeth, the urge to see how Georgiana did had become nearly as strong. To Pemberley he would go.

But Darcy's homecoming was hardly what he'd anticipated. He'd entered Pemberley's grounds just past nightfall after travelling for three long, arduous days. The torches that lined the gravel drive burned brightly in welcome, a familiar sight that made the heaviness of his heart a little lighter, as did the figure of Colonel Fitzwilliam, who threw open the door with a wide grin the moment Darcy alighted from the carriage and ascended the front steps. They exchanged pleasantries and, though Darcy desired to see Georgiana directly, he obliged Richard by joining him for a drink in his private sitting room, where the colonel promptly poured Pemberley's master a healthy glass of brandy, and none for himself.

It was then that Darcy made several observations, the first being his cousin's complexion. For an athletic officer in Her Majesty's Army well-known to spend far more time out-of-doors than in, Richard appeared exceptionally pale, even in the dimly lit interior. Certainly, he hadn't spent the last several months at Pemberley lounging about indoors! Darcy took a fortifying drink and proceeded to tease him about it, which led to a second and third observation: Richard's uncharacteristic seriousness, and a smile that didn't reach his eyes.

In that moment Darcy feared something terrible had happened, either to or concerning Georgiana, but before he could form the words something else caught his eye, the very possibility of which chilled him to the bone. The proof was there, however, staring him in the face. Darcy's glass slipped from his hand and shattered upon the hearth. The colonel cringed, but held his cousin's horrified gaze with a slightly sheepish expression. Instead of a brilliant, piercing blue, Richard's eyes were now dark like Georgiana's, like Elizabeth's and Mr. Bennet's.

"It's not your fault," Colonel Fitzwilliam said as Darcy shuddered, attempting to shake off the unpleasantness and discomfort that particular memory never failed to invoke.

"When you left for Hertfordshire—at Georgiana's urging, I might add—we had no idea she was still relatively unstable; certainly not to the extent that she was. She'd adjusted far better than either of us had expected her to once we'd returned to Pemberley from Ramsgate, and she hadn't shown any outward behavior that indicated we ought to be overly concerned. Since then, both of us have learned to read her better. As for me, I'm perfectly well."

"Perfectly well," Darcy parroted, his countenance dark. "She was a fifteen-year-old girl whose judgment was anything but sound *before* she became a *vampyre*. I never should have left you or my staff alone with her!"

"And I fail to see how things would have been any better had you actually been here. In a moment of weakness, she probably would have done the same to you."

"Would to God that she had, then!" he hollered, his voice raw with emotion.

The colonel stared at him long and hard. There were no secrets between them. Richard knew all about Elizabeth and the depth of Darcy's devotion to her, as well as her refusal to be with his cousin in any capacity, and her reasons why. "Darcy," he said gently, "you know you are not entirely without options."

Darcy clenched his jaw and shook his head, his expression nothing short of tortured. "Becoming what she is…it's *not* an option, Richard, not so long as I retain my health and my sanity."

"You consider yourself in good health, do you? And sane?" The colonel laughed humourlessly. "You hardly sleep at night and of late I've seen you consume more brandy than you have food. That is anything but healthy. If you continue in this vein you will drive yourself to an early grave. Surely, Miss Bennet did not risk her reputation and that of her family in order to save your life in Hertfordshire, only to have you slowly kill yourself in Derbyshire. She wouldn't want this for you."

Darcy pounded his fist upon his desk. "She wants nothing of me!" he cried. "Nothing at all!"

"That remains to be seen. In the meantime, tell me precisely what it is that *you* want, Cousin, for you cannot continue to carry on as you have been. You do yourself—and those who care for you—great harm."

Darcy pressed the heels of his hands into his eyes. "Her," he breathed. "To be with her. Nothing more, nothing less, but it is hopeless, Richard. So long as I am human she will never consent to have me. She will never consent to come here to Pemberley, or become my wife."

"Yet she loves you."

Darcy exhaled raggedly. "So she says."

"And you will not consider…changing. Not even for her?"

Darcy closed his eyes, his chest tight as he resolutely shook his head. "Not so long as I am in health. I have too many responsibilities, too many people who depend upon me for their livelihood and well-being. I could not bear to put them at such a risk."

"And what if you were not in health?" Fitzwilliam asked.

Darcy swallowed thickly. "If my health was failing due to illness or if I were injured…" he began hoarsely. "If there was absolutely no other option— no glimmer of hope for my recovery—then I suppose that would be a different matter."

Fitzwilliam raised one brow. "You would consent, then? To become what Miss Bennet is— what Georgiana and I are—if that was the only option left to you, aside from death?"

The master of Pemberley was silent for a long while. "If I were truly dying, Richard, and I could be with Elizabeth—always, and never be parted from her—then yes," he said, meeting his cousin's eyes. "I would give you my consent."

Ten

"Leave it alone, Georgiana, I will not discuss such things with you."

Darcy's tone was harsh as he led his horse from the stable and into the yard, where he wasted no time climbing into the saddle and quick-shortening the reins. He had no patience for questions, particularly from his sister, who'd boldly broached a subject she should know nothing about: namely, Elizabeth Bennet. Clearly, he would have to have a discussion with Richard later about loyalty and discretion.

Georgiana rushed forward, blocking his path and startling his horse. The stallion tossed its head and squealed as it side-stepped toward the gravel drive and tugged against the reins, dangerously close to rearing.

"Georgiana," he snapped, struggling to keep the skittish animal under control. Most of Pemberley's horses didn't appreciate having vampyres in their midst. There were a half dozen or so who, for the most part, tolerated Georgiana's and Richard's presence—and a few who even acquiesced to being ridden by them—but this particular horse wasn't one of those. He was fast, though, and high spirited— exactly what Darcy's foul mood required this morning.

"I'm sorry, Fitzwilliam, but I'm worried about you. Everyone is worried about you." She clasped her hands together and gazed up at him with dark, serious eyes—eyes that used to be blue, like their late mother's.

Darcy regarded her for a long moment, his irritation slowly ebbing. "I know," he muttered, turning his head aside and squinting toward the eastern fields, where he planned to spend the next hour tearing across the estate on horseback, exercising his demons. "It wasn't my intention to make you worry. Pray forgive me."

"You know I will do whatever you ask of me," she assured him in a quiet voice. "Anything at all…"

"Georgiana…" he warned.

"*Please,* Brother. I would never judge you. No one will, so please, will you not simply tell me what I may do for you so that you'll be happy again?"

"Nothing," he said tightly, his temper flaring once more. He knew full well that she was one of the few who *could* help him—and would, for that matter—but her assistance in that quarter was absolutely out of the question. Not only did he not want such a thing to weigh upon her young conscience, but Darcy's responsibilities to the people of Pemberley and his sense of familial duty rested far too heavily upon his shoulders to simply allow his personal desires to take precedence over his accountability.

Not to mention the more he thought about actually exploring such an option, the more anxious and agitated he became. The more anxious and agitated he became, the more inclined he was to reject that option altogether. It wasn't immortality he wanted in any case, but Elizabeth.

Darcy clenched his jaw. In only a few short months Richard appeared to have embraced his accidental vampirism with startling ease and acceptance. In fact, his sunny attitude and sense of humour were so reminiscent of Elizabeth's good-natured disposition that Darcy could no longer bear to be in his company for any length of time. The throb of longing in his breast was too painful. His cousin's animation and ability to tease made Darcy literally ache to be with the raven-haired beauty who'd stolen his heart; but she'd refused him and had fled to London. He hadn't seen, nor heard word of her since, not even from Bingley, who was now married to her eldest sister.

Like Colonel Fitzwilliam, Georgiana seemed to have found her stride as well. She could finally be trusted to wander through the house and grounds unaccompanied, though she often preferred a companion. More often than not it was Richard, who always went out of his way to bring a smile to her face or make her laugh, usually at Darcy's expense.

The fact of the matter was that Darcy's cousin and sister appeared to be thriving as vampyres. But what if Darcy underwent the same metamorphosis and didn't thrive? What if he finally took a leap of faith and became like Elizabeth, only to discover—after the fact—that he was nothing like her at all? What if he turned into a blood-thirsty monster and retained absolutely no shred of his staunch self-control? What if he ended up slaying every human being he came in contact with, including those in his care and under his protection? Would Elizabeth be angry with him? Would she be disgusted and disappointed? Would she tell him she wanted nothing to do with him ever again and order him away? Darcy didn't think he could survive a second rejection, or the possibility of harming anyone so barbarously, especially after having made such a permanent, life-altering commitment. The consequences were not only terrifying, but everlasting; infinite and unalterable.

How on earth would he ever live with himself?

Darcy ran his hand over his mouth and shut his eyes, expelling a ragged breath. His sister stood several meters away, a respectful distance so as not to further unsettle his horse. Georgiana's care and concern for him were genuine, as was her almost desperate desire to see him happy. At the tender age of fifteen she'd endured enough pain and regret to last a lifetime—and last a lifetime it would, and more. With Darcy and Richard to care for her, however—and maybe, someday, God willing, with Elizabeth as her friend—perhaps she wouldn't see her past as regretful. Perhaps her future would be bright, joyful, and brimming with promise.

The corners of Darcy's mouth lifted slightly as he envisioned his sister and Elizabeth together. As usual, the sensation of satisfaction he felt from indulging such a heartfelt fantasy was fleeting, leaving him with a profound emptiness and deep sense of loss. Darcy opened his eyes and shifted his gaze to Georgiana, who regarded him with furrowed brows as he swallowed thickly and cleared his throat.

"I'll be fine, Georgiana. I may not be at the moment, but I will be at some point. Now, be merciful and allow me the sanctity of my morning ride before Richard decides to join me. His incessant chatter always grates on my horse's nerves."

Georgiana pursed her lips. "Very well, Fitzwilliam. I hereby release you, but only to spare your poor horse a headache." This earned a genuine smile from her brother, which quickly faded when she added, "I am not so easily dissuaded, you know. We *will* discuss this."

Darcy shook his head with a scowl.

"If Miss Bennet truly makes you happy," she continued defiantly, "if you *love* her, Brother, then you must know I'd want to know her—especially if she's like me."

It was too much, by far too much. Furious with this new, outspoken version of his sister, not to mention Richard for poisoning her mind with faerie tales that could never come to fruition, Darcy snapped the reins and dug his heels into his horse's sides. He barely heard Georgiana's hasty cry, imploring him to be careful.

Darcy snorted contemptuously. At the moment he certainly didn't feel like being careful. In fact, the master of Pemberley had a fierce urge to be as spiteful and obstinate as his sister was willful. Leaning low over his mount, he flew over the countryside at a punishing pace. The adrenaline pumping through his body combined with the high rate of speed at which he was travelling made him feel invincible, as though nothing and no one in the entire universe could possibly conquer him.

A fallen tree choked by thick, twisted vines lay in his path, but his horse cleared it as though it were nothing more than a branch or even a twig. A hedge, a fence, a mound of earth, a boulder, a rock wall— all were hurdled with little effort. It was exhilarating, and Darcy revelled in every soul-freeing second of his rebellion.

Just ahead a wooded grove loomed, its ancient trees sentient and still. It bordered a natural spring-fed lake, a favorite spot for fishing in the summer months; one Darcy had frequented on horseback from the time he was a young boy. He knew the path well, and his intent was to guide his mount through the dense maze of timber without slowing his pace; but as they neared the tree line his stallion began pulling against the reins and tossing his head. Darcy tightened his grip and fought to retain control, but his horse had other ideas. The ornery animal stopped short, reared, bucked, and threw his master a half dozen meters. Darcy landed hard upon the frozen ground.

There he lay, unmoving; flat on his back as he laboured to draw breath. The sheer force of his landing caused his head to reel, his ears to ring, and bright white blotches of light to pulse painfully behind his eyes. Weakened and nearly overcome by the pain in his skull, he turned his eyes heavenward, where the mid-morning sky was a deep, almost impossible shade of blue. The color, as so many things had since he'd met her, reminded him immediately of Elizabeth, or, more particularly, of a gown she'd once worn in his presence. The rich cerulean muslin had looked exquisite against her pale skin, so exquisite in fact that he'd found it extremely difficult at the time to refrain from touching her bare shoulders, or her neck, or any other part of her that was exposed to him. Somehow, though, he'd managed to remain a gentleman. It was something that, even in his current, decidedly grim state, Fitzwilliam Darcy of Pemberley could not bring himself to regret. His only regret was that he hadn't tried harder to win her; that he hadn't followed her to London and courted her relentlessly, until she was as passionately in love with him as he was with her and no longer of a mind to refuse him anything. But now, as he lay sprawled upon the cold ground unable to move, he knew that any chance of reuniting with Elizabeth was lost to him. She was lost to him forever.

Darcy groaned as the pain in his head increased to an intolerable level, but so, too, had the acute discomfort spreading through his chest. Whether the latter was from constantly yearning for the woman he loved these past months or from any physical injuries he sustained after his horse had thrown him, Darcy was in no condition to discern.

With a ragged exhalation he shut his eyes tightly and gritted his teeth against the absolute agony seizing his body. It was quickly overpowering him, pulling him with thorny fingers and eager arms into a dark, velvety abyss where Darcy knew nothing, and felt nothing. Not even the pain of his broken heart.

Eleven

Darcy combed his fingers through his hair, exhaling heavily as he stood in Longbourn's finest drawing room. Six months had passed since he'd last been in Hertfordshire; half a year since he'd seen Elizabeth. So much had happened in that span of time. *Too much,* he thought as his mouth twisted ruefully.

The anticipation of finally seeing her again, coupled with the agitation he felt regarding the obvious differences in his appearance, was enough to drive him out of his mind. Darcy needed a distraction and strode to the nearest window, where he was afforded a picturesque view of the Bennets' small park. The weather was fair—partly sunny and dry, if not a bit chilly for late spring—and he wondered whether Elizabeth would consent to walk out with him, preferably without a chaperone. He'd be foolish to think she wouldn't have questions the moment she laid eyes on him, and figured it would be far better for both of them if they had no audience under foot.

His injuries from his accident had been severe, so severe in fact that Colonel Fitzwilliam had immediately sent to London for a physician, but it'd made little difference in the end. Though his lacerations faded with time and his broken bones had begun to mend, Darcy never regained consciousness. After a month passed with no sign of improvement, his sister, who flatly refused to leave his sickbed, was instructed to prepare for the inevitable. Richard was grieved, but Georgiana had been inconsolable. By the time Darcy's heartbeat had grown so faint it could barely be detected, she'd borne all she possibly could. Richard hadn't even tried to stop her.

Darcy's hand went instinctively to his neck, where two small puncture wounds were once visible. They'd faded almost instantly after his change, but would have been concealed in any case, neatly hidden beneath his shirt collar and the artfully tied layers of his cravat. He hadn't felt Georgiana's bite—not even so much as a pinch—but the pain that followed was vivid still, burned into his memory as though with a branding iron. The sheer agony of it had consumed him, raging in his body for an entire day before gradually receding to nothing more than the minor discomfort of a sore throat.

His thirst was always with him, but to his immense relief it by no means ruled him or defined who he was. As it turned out, the well-practiced self-control Darcy had so prided himself upon throughout his nine-and-twenty years as a human proved an asset to him still. Not only had the master of Pemberley learned to resist the mouth-watering lure of human blood, but he'd become adept at ignoring the incessant burn in his throat as well.

Sighing heavily, he laid his forehead against the window and closed his eyes. It was nearly tea time, and the room he occupied faced the east, untouched by the late afternoon sun. The smooth panes, however, weren't cool to his touch, but felt almost warm. He still wasn't quite accustomed to that; to his body's temperature being either lower than or equal to that of inanimate objects. He recalled the first time he'd grasped Georgiana's hand in his after he'd awoken from his transformation and smiled. By then, Darcy was so used to feeling the chill of death whenever he touched her that he hadn't expected her skin to feel warm to him. It'd come as a shock, but it didn't follow that shock was unwelcome. It was tangible evidence they were the same once again; the same temperature and the same type of entity. Brother and sister still, yet bound by so much more than the blood of their birth.

The slamming of a door above stairs roused him from his reverie, the unmistakable sound of footsteps on the staircase alerting him to the fact that he would soon have company. Much to Darcy's disappointment and annoyance, it was not the light staccato cadence of a lady's, but the heavier footfalls of a gentleman. With a sigh of resignation, he straightened his shoulders and waited patiently for Elizabeth's father, choosing to keep his back to the room as he stared fixedly out of the window. When the drawing room door was thrown open a moment later, the master of Pemberley remained as he was, and therefore sensed rather than saw Mr. Bennet enter.

"Mr. Darcy," he said icily and without preamble. "I thought I made it perfectly clear to you the last time you were in Hertfordshire that your presence is neither desired, nor welcomed in my home."

Darcy took a fortifying breath and turned to greet Elizabeth's father, gratified to see the expression of anger on the elder man's face quickly transformed to one of shock as he observed Darcy's altered appearance.

"How do you do, Mr. Bennet?" he asked cordially, pleased with himself for managing to keep any hint of smugness from his tone.

Mr. Bennet gaped at him before scrambling to shut the door. "Are you mad?" he hissed. "What in God's name have you done?"

"I am not a frivolous man, Mr. Bennet. Nothing has been done that was not strictly necessary, I assure you."

"*Necessary...!* Young man, I am not accustomed to being trifled with. However insincere you choose to be, you will not find me so. If this is some drastic ploy to manipulate my second daughter into bestowing her favour upon you, I can promise you will be grievously disappointed, not to mention exceedingly sorry once I've finished with you."

Darcy stiffened. "Hardly," he responded, his tone curt. "I merely fell from my horse."

"You fell from your horse," Mr. Bennet parroted condescendingly.

"I did. It was a most unfortunate accident, but hardly out of the ordinary. Plenty of perfectly capable horsemen and women are often thrown from their mounts. In fact, when I was last in Hertfordshire Miss Elizabeth informed me she'd once fallen from her own horse, and that you were so deeply grieved by the severity of her injuries that you oversaw her recovery personally."

The elder man's eyes narrowed. "What *exactly* did my daughter tell you about her accident, *sir?*"

"More than enough," Darcy said with a pointed look. "Contrary to what you may think, Mr. Bennet,

I've no desire to quarrel with you about the events that transpired between you and your daughter three years ago. That wasn't my intent in coming here today. My intent—"

"Your intent, Mr. Darcy, is undoubtedly to blackmail me into allowing you to have my daughter!"

Darcy's mouth twisted with distaste. "I have no wish to expose you and your family—your second daughter especially—any more than I wish exposure upon myself and my own." *Good God, the man is impossible!*

Running his hand over his mouth, Darcy paced the length of the room impatiently as he debated how much or how little he should reveal to Mr. Bennet concerning *his* family, namely Georgiana and Richard. At length, he decided complete honesty was his best course, or else he'd most likely be in danger of facing an eternity of hostility and false accusations from a man he very much hoped would one day become his father-in-law.

Standing before the fire, Darcy propped his elbows upon the mantle and rubbed the back of his neck with his hand. The steady heat of the flames licking at the logs in the grate warmed him, reminding him of countless pleasant nights passed in front of the hearths at Pemberley. A bright, crackling fire was a novelty to him now rather than a necessity, but for appearance sake the tradition must be maintained, lest suspicions be raised. "Has your daughter confided anything to you about my own family?" he inquired lowly.

Mr. Bennet pursed his lips sourly and shook his head.

"If I may, I'd like to tell you about them."

After taking several moments to consider Darcy's request, Mr. Bennet indicated two upholstered chairs before the hearth with an exaggerated sweep of his arm. "By all means," he replied with a patronizing tone. "I suppose it's only fair, since you seem to know so much about mine."

Willing his irritation to dissipate, Darcy settled into a chair and cleared his throat while Elizabeth's father claimed the other, drumming his fingers impatiently upon the arms of his chair and raising an expectant brow. In that moment the elder man's expression reminded Darcy very much of Elizabeth, but the moment was fleeting.

"I was angry with my sister and riding rather recklessly," he began, purposely meeting Mr. Bennet's challenging gaze, "when my horse threw me. While the broken bones I suffered weren't life-threatening, the injury I sustained to my head was another matter. I lay abed for many weeks, comatose, unresponsive, with no sign of improvement. Georgiana, I was told, never left my side.

"There was nothing to be done, however. My prognosis was extremely grim, and eventually my already poor condition began to deteriorate even further. In what ought to have been my final moments, Georgiana exerted what means were within her power in order to preserve me from true death. It was thereby done, and done for the best."

The elder man regarded Darcy with furrowed brows and shook his head. "I don't understand," he muttered, but it wasn't long before comprehension dawned and Mr. Bennet jerked to the edge of his seat. "Your *sister*...?" he cried incredulously. "You mean to tell me your *sister,* who cannot be more than sixteen years of age, has been immortalized?"

"Yes," Darcy replied somberly, "Georgiana is a vampyre, and has been for nearly a year. Had she not acted to save me, I'm quite certain my cousin would have in her stead. While Georgiana's intent was undoubtedly to prolong the life of a brother she'd long considered more of a father figure, Richard has been my confident since we were children. He was well acquainted with the depth of my feelings for Miss Elizabeth, as well as the impossibilities attached to our situation and the depth of my despair at the time. If *he* had acted, it would not have been to save my life, per se, but to give me a chance to have a future with your daughter; a future I very much desired but was convinced I would never have."

Mr. Bennet exhaled roughly and scrubbed his hands over his face. "Does Elizabeth know anything of your sister and cousin?"

"I've spoken to her about my sister, yes, but I wasn't aware of Richard's transformation until after I returned to Pemberley last November. When I'd left Derbyshire for Netherfield Georgiana was still relatively…unreliable, if you will, although neither Richard nor I realized the true extent of the risk she posed at the time. All things considered, they've both adjusted remarkably well since then, Richard especially. His outlook is much like your daughter's, as is his sense of humour. Through it all, he's retained his ability to tease."

"I can well imagine your frustration, then," Mr. Bennet said dryly, linking his fingers over his stomach as he relaxed his posture and reclined in his chair.

Darcy bowed his head and leaned forward to rest his elbows upon his knees. "I assure you that you cannot," he said quietly. "I daresay no one can. The three people I'd come to cherish most in the world were vampyres. Out of the three, only two wanted anything to do with me so long as I remained human. Miss Elizabeth would not consider changing me and, so long as I was in health, neither was I willing to be changed. Not by her, my sister, or my cousin, though I knew Georgiana and Richard were more than willing to assist in that quarter. Your daughter and I were at a stalemate."

"You've come to court her, then. Even after the inhospitable way I treated you last autumn. I have to say, I'm impressed."

"With all due respect, Mr. Bennet, your impression of me is of little import to me at this juncture. Your ill-treatment of me last autumn was beyond inhospitable. Rather than bothering to get to know me, you chose instead to treat me with contempt, which not only injured me, but your daughter, who, out of the goodness of her heart, did nothing more than offer me her friendship." Darcy exhaled roughly and ran his hand over his mouth. "To be perfectly honest, I've little interest in *courting* Miss Elizabeth."

Mr. Bennet removed his glasses and rubbed his eyes. "If you had a beautiful, young daughter who happened to be a *vampyre*, Mr. Darcy," he said tightly, "who was knowingly entangling herself with a human male—a mortal—who not only had no idea *what* she was, but what sort of danger she posed to him, perhaps then you'd better comprehend my reluctance to place my trust in either of you so freely."

Darcy's temper flared and, before he could check himself, said hotly, "*My sister* is more than ten years my junior. In my absence last summer she was transformed from an innocent, carefree *human* girl into a veritable monster by the worst kind of fortune-hunter. In an instant her hopes—nay, her entire future *and mine*—were dashed to hell, so believe me when I say I'm well aware of the potential threats posed by a persistent suitor!" He leapt from his chair and strode to the opposite side of the room.

It was then that the drawing room door was opened with a quiet click of its brass handle. Instinctively, Darcy turned toward the sound, his breath catching almost painfully in his throat as Elizabeth entered amongst a flurry of dark curls and pale, pink silk. She looked as beautiful as ever as her fiery gaze settled, not on her father, but directly upon him. Darcy swallowed thickly and willed himself to remain where he was rather than crossing the room to drop to his knees at her feet. Her name was on the tip of his tongue but, to his consternation, Mr. Bennet's voice preceded his.

"Elizabeth, what on earth do you think you're doing, child?" Mr. Bennet demanded, rising from his chair.

"I'd like to speak with Mr. Darcy, Father, regarding a matter most urgent."

Twelve

"I'm afraid that's out of the question," Mr. Bennet replied, striding toward his daughter and taking her hand in his. "Why don't you return above stairs, my dear, and leave the two of us to our discussion. You and I can talk later, after Mr. Darcy has gone."

But Elizabeth refused to be summarily dismissed. She retracted her hand from his grasp and spoke firmly. "I'm sorry, Papa, but what I have to say to Mr. Darcy cannot be put off until later. It must be said now."

"Elizabeth," her father said lowly, "you will do as I say. You must."

"Have I not always done what you've asked of me, regardless of whether your decisions have brought me happiness or disappointment," she inquired, looking him determinedly in the eye, "regardless of whether your requests were something I wished to comply with or not?"

"You have," he conceded, "but—"

"I would like to speak with Mr. Darcy, sir."

"Lizzy—"

"No, Papa. I deserve to know happiness! I deserve it just as much as Jane, for I have as much soul as she, and full as much heart. It may no longer beat within my breast, but I assure you it is there, and it aches."

Though a flash of compassion appeared in Mr. Bennet's eyes, his countenance remained grim. "Elizabeth, we cannot give our neighbours any reason to suspect what we are. You know this, yet you insist upon arguing with me. It is very much out of character for you to defy me, especially when the safety of our family is at stake."

"Our neighbours," Elizabeth repeated bitterly. "I've grown tired of always considering our neighbours. You know as well as I that our neighbours will always find something to talk about so far as our family is concerned. Forgive me, but Mamma has seen to that many times, as have my younger sisters, yet it's never their behavior you see fit to check, but my own. I've done nothing wrong."

"Of course you haven't my dear," her father chided, reaching once more for her hand, "but your mother's and sisters' antics are quite effective in drawing attention away from both of us. You know that, and we must therefore use it to our advantage."

Elizabeth snatched her hand away and folded her arms across her breasts. "No, sir, I know no such thing. If anything, their unchecked behaviour invites scrutiny and gossip, and always will. Do you honestly think our neighbours failed to notice the differences in my appearance since I was injured nearly four years ago? Do you think they don't speculate about that or your own alterations—or lack thereof—even now? That they would have been so busy observing Jane with Mr. Bingley and the foolishness of Mary, Kitty, and Lydia last autumn that we would have gone unobserved ourselves? You know that we would not have. You know that we would have been watched just as closely, perhaps more so owing to our penchant for restraint."

Mr. Bennet's ire grew. "Elizabeth, your attention to Mr. Darcy and his to you put us at serious risk—"

"No. My friendship with Mr. Darcy might have turned a few heads and incited some idle talk, but only of the usual variety. You were afraid, Papa. You recognized his admiration for me, and shortly after that, mine for him.

"At first you were afraid I would end up harming him—or worse—but once you began to realise Mr. Darcy was in no danger from me you became frightened; frightened I might wish to leave with him rather than remain at Longbourn with you, and that eventually you would be alone."

Silence followed, and Mr. Bennet paced stiffly to the window, where he remained for many minutes, staring at the same view of the park Darcy had earlier. Eventually, Elizabeth went to him. The words they exchanged were quiet now; too quiet for even Darcy's keen ears to discern.

At last Mr. Bennet sighed tiredly. "The last thing I wanted was to cause you unhappiness, Lizzy, but it appears I have. I thought at first…" but the elder man's voice trailed off as he shook his head sadly. He glanced at Darcy, his eyes suspiciously moist, and cleared his throat. "You may do what you will," he said quietly, "both of you." He inclined his head to Darcy and, without another word, strode from the room, leaving the door ajar behind him.

Elizabeth remained at the window, her head bowed and her hands clasped in front of her. Darcy took a fortifying breath and joined her, standing so close that he could smell her scent. He closed his eyes and inhaled deeply. She was exactly as he remembered her—in every way—and she was finally close enough to touch. Against his better judgment he leaned forward, fully intending to throw caution to the wind and finally place his lips upon her neck, but she turned before he had the chance.

"You are like me," she whispered, her eyes intent upon his face.

"I am," he replied as he struggled to rein in his desire to kiss her.

She lifted her hand, as though to touch him, then hesitated and let it drop to her side. "Did you do this for me?"

The corner of Darcy's mouth lifted as he grasped her hand with his own and placed it upon his chest, over his dormant heart and held it there. "I did not; although, I confess I might have given my cousin leave to do with me what he would should I ever find myself in a life-threatening predicament. In the end, however, it was Georgiana who took matters into her own hands." They regarded each other for a long moment until Darcy could no longer bear her silence. "Are you disappointed?" he whispered anxiously.

Elizabeth dipped her head and closed her eyes. Her dark lashes were so long they brushed her cheeks, and Darcy could not but admire the contrast; the inky blackness of her lashes against the paleness of her flesh. As if she wasn't appealing enough, one lone curl escaped the confines of her jewelled comb to gently caress the column of her neck. Darcy exhaled shakily.

"No," she replied, gazing at him through her lashes, "quite the opposite. I'm a selfish being, though. I wished often for a solution so that we might finally be together, but I never wished harm to come to you. I never wanted you to be in any danger."

Darcy drew her closer and, to his great delight, Elizabeth allowed him to hold her in his arms. He laid his cheek upon the top of her head and closed his eyes. "I know," he breathed, "but in the end perhaps my desire to be with you was simply too great."

She inhaled sharply and attempted to pull away, but Darcy tightened his hold upon her and buried his face in the crook of her neck. "I fear I am selfish as well. Though I didn't mean to be, I'd grown increasingly reckless whenever I went out riding, and chose horses from my stable well known for their spirited temperaments. At the time, I attributed my increasingly foul moods to my restlessness, and to my ever-constant state of discontent. I lived with my sister and cousin, both of whom are vampyres—immortal, like you. I saw them every day, spent time with them, spoke with them, yet I'd never felt so alone in my entire life. How I missed you!" he whispered fiercely. "Though I lived and breathed, I felt dead inside. Nothing I did, save for racing across Pemberley's grounds at break-neck speeds, made me feel alive. How I wanted you, Elizabeth!"

"And I you," she whispered, her words catching in her throat. "I hoped you'd come for me when I went to London—I prayed that you would—but you did not. I told myself it was for the best, but I burned for you, every single day."

"I realize that now," he said. "If I'd have known for certain I would have walked there—crawled there on my hands and knees from Derbyshire—but you'd already refused me and told me not to follow you." He shook his head. "I should have followed my heart instead. I should have gone to London and declared myself again, and again, and again, until you either accepted me or sent me away forever."

"You're here now."

"Yes," he said, "and so I shall remain. As long as we exist I'll stay by your side. I swear it."

To Darcy's dismay, Elizabeth suddenly released him, but any alarm he felt lasted no longer than an instant as her fingertips traced the line of his jaw with such tenderness Darcy thought he might burst from happiness. The look in her eyes as she gazed at him was one of undeniable adoration and love.

With a smile, he tucked an errant curl behind her ear and turned his cheek, gently kissing her palm. "Elizabeth," he sighed, irrevocably and incandescently happy at last. "Dearest, loveliest, Elizabeth!"

Several tears escaped from beneath her lashes and Elizabeth bit her lip, closing her eyes as she exhaled unsteadily.

Darcy dipped his head and kissed them tenderly from her cheeks.

She swallowed convulsively. "My dearest sir," she said, her voice barely above a whisper, "you must allow me to tell you how ardently I admire and love you."

His lips were swift as they descended upon hers, and suffice it to say, Darcy knew.

About the Author

Susan Adriani has been an admirer of Jane Austen and her beloved characters for over twenty years. Originally from New England, she attended a small fine arts college, where she majored in Illustration. In 2007, after contemplating the unexplored possibilities in one of Jane Austen's most celebrated novels, *Pride and Prejudice*, Ms. Adriani laid aside her paintbrush and began to write her first novel-length story, *The Truth About Mr. Darcy*. With encouragement from fellow Austen enthusiasts she continued. Ms. Adriani currently resides in Connecticut with her husband, daughter, and a very impertinent cat.

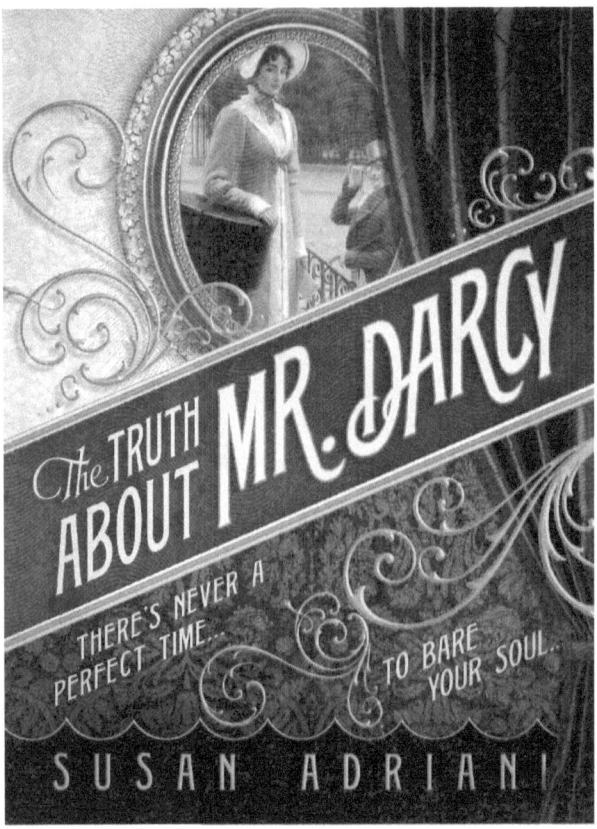

The Truth Always Has Consequences . . . .

Mr. Darcy has a dilemma. Should he tell the truth about his old nemesis George Wickham in order to protect the good citizens of Meryton from Wickham's lies and deceits? Doing so will force Darcy to reveal family secrets that he'd prefer never come to light. The alternative is keeping the man's criminal nature to himself and hoping he leaves the area before doing significant harm.

But as Wickham's attentions to Elizabeth increase, Darcy knows if he's to win the one woman he's set his heart on, he's going to have to make one of the most difficult decisions of his life. And what he ultimately does sets in motion a shocking train of events neither he nor Elizabeth could possibly have predicted.

  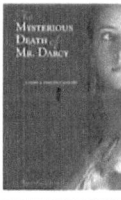  

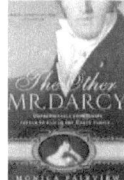